FASTBALL FEVER

Other Books by Anna Durand

Fastball Fever (All-American Men, Book One)
One Hot Chance (Hot Brits, Book One)
One Hot Roomie (Hot Brits, Book Two)
One Hot Crush (Hot Brits, Book Three)
The Dixon Brothers Trilogy (Hot Brits, Books 1-3 + Bonus Chapters)
One Hot Escape (Hot Brits, Book Four)
One Hot Rumor (Hot Brits, Book Five)
One Hot Christmas (Hot Brits, Book Six)
One Hot Scandal (Hot Brits, Book Seven)
One Hot Deal (Hot Brits, Book Eight)
One Hot Favor (Hot Brits, Book Nine)
One Hot Bash (Hot Brits, Book Ten)
One Hot Moment (Hot Brits, Book Eleven)
One Hot Chase (Hot Brits, Book Twelve)
The American Wives Club (A Hot Brits/Hot Scots/Au Naturel Crossover)
Brit vs. Scot (A Hot Brits/Hot Scots/Au Naturel Crossover)
A Novel Secret (A Hot Brits/Hot Scots/Au Naturel Crossover)
Dangerous in a Kilt (Hot Scots, Book One)
Wicked in a Kilt (Hot Scots, Book Two)
Scandalous in a Kilt (Hot Scots, Book Three)
The MacTaggart Brothers Trilogy (Hot Scots, Books 1-3)
Gift-Wrapped in a Kilt (Hot Scots, Book Four)
Notorious in a Kilt (Hot Scots, Book Five)
Insatiable in a Kilt (Hot Scots, Book Six)
Lethal in a Kilt (Hot Scots, Book Seven)
Irresistible in a Kilt (Hot Scots, Book Eight)
Devastating in a Kilt (Hot Scots, Book Nine)
Spellbound in a Kilt (Hot Scots, Book Ten)
Relentless in a Kilt (Hot Scots, Book Eleven)
Incendiary in a Kilt (Hot Scots, Book Twelve)
Wild in a Kilt (Hot Scots, Book Thirteen)
Unstoppable in a Kilt (Hot Scots, Book Fourteen)
Valentine in a Kilt (Hot Scots, Book Fifteen)
Electrifying in a Kilt (Hot Scots, Book Sixteen)
The Notorious Dr. MacT (A Hot Scots Prequel)
The British Bastard (A Hot Scots Prequel)
Natural Obsession (Au Naturel Nights, Book One)
Natural Deception (Au Naturel Nights, Book Two)
Natural Temptation (Au Naturel Nights, Book Three)
Natural Passion (Au Naturel Trilogy, Book One)
Natural Impulse (Au Naturel Trilogy, Book Two)
Natural Satisfaction (Au Naturel Trilogy, Book Three)
Lachlan in a Kilt (The Ballachulish Trilogy, Book One)
Aidan in a Kilt (The Ballachulish Trilogy, Book Two)
Rory in a Kilt (The Ballachulish Trilogy, Book Three)

All-American Men, Book One

JACOBSVILLE BOOKS JB CHESTERHILL, OHIO

FASTBALL FEVER

ISBN: 978-1-964417-43-1 (paperback)
ISBN: 978-1-964417-44-8 (ebook)
ISBN: 978-1-964417-45-5 (retail audiobook)
ISBN: 978-1-964417-46-2 (library audiobook)

Library of Congress Control Number: 2025913014

Manufactured in the United States.

Jacobsville Books
www.JacobsvilleBooks.com

Publisher's Cataloging-in-Publication Data
provided by Five Rainbows Cataloging Services

Names: Durand, Anna.
Title: Fastball fever / Anna Durand.
Description: Chesterhill, OH : Jacobsville Books, 2025. | Series: All-American men, bk. 1.
Identifiers: ISBN 978-1-964417-43-1 (paperback) | ISBN 978-1-964417-44-8 (ebook) | ISBN 978-1-964417-45-5 (retail audiobook) | 978-1-964417-46-2 (library audiobook)
Subjects: LCSH: Baseball players--Fiction. | Sports injuries--Fiction. | Women coaches (Athletics)--Fiction. | World Series (Baseball)--Fiction. | Man-woman relationships--Fiction. | Romance fiction. | BISAC: FICTION / Romance / Sports. | FICTION / Romance / Contemporary. | FICTION / Romance / Workplace. | GSAFD: Love stories.
Classification: LCC PS3604.U724 F37 2025 (print) | LCC PS3604.U724 (ebook) | DDC 813/.6--dc23.

Chapter One

The Fall From Grace

The humid Florida air wraps around me like a sufhe humid Florida air wraps around me like a suffocating glove as I stride onto the mound at Jacksonville's Admirals stadium. The air is alive with restless cheers and the occasional whistle. The people are waiting for me—for my fastball to blast Nolan Ryan's record to smithereens. Sweat clings to my skin, fusing my uniform to my back, but I ignore it. As I zero in on home plate, the aroma of salt drifts in from the ocean miles away. I can smell the asphalt from the parking lot too.

How long has it taken me to get to this moment? Years. My steadfast training and determination brought me to this day in this stadium. I've been waiting for it all my life, that's how it feels to me.

This is a no-brainer, kid. Shatter that record. Then you can move on to destroying Aroldis Chapman's fastest pitch too.

Piece of cake.

Now it's time for the windup.

I position my feet shoulder-width apart and raise my hands to chest height, getting ready for the pitch. A gentle sway follows. I step forward at a forty-five-degree angle, allowing my hips to pivot slightly while my right foot rotates inward to align along the rubber.

From the corner of my eye, I catch Jared Morris charging down the line, smirking like the jackass he is.

The crowd, they're here for me, roaring and chanting as if I've already won the game. They're cheering for the new fastball king—for me, Charlie Braddock. But I haven't even thrown the ball yet. My pulse races in anticipation. But that doesn't matter. I won't let it matter. So, I stare straight ahead at the catcher's mitt, blocking out the noise of the crowd. My arm aches just a little, enough to remind me that I'm not the twenty-one-year-old I used to be, not anymore. I ignore the thought and focus on the pitch that will change my future and make me into a legend.

Aiming. Concentrating. My gaze narrows as I run through the motions in my head, owning the moment before I pitch that ball for real. The dirt shifts beneath my cleats. An insect buzzes past my ear. The weight of the stadium seems to bear down on me—in a good way. The entire stadium is holding its breath in anticipation, and so am I.

It's now or never, and never's not an option.

A strange sensation ripples through me, and I swear I can hear Nolan Ryan breathing down my neck from whatever Texas ranch he's hiding out on these days. I wouldn't mind if he could hear the sound of my fastball whizzing past him. It'll put me on top of the list of fastball legends. After eleven years in the majors, I'm on the cusp of achieving the dream. The kid who grew up in the Iowa cornfields can do something more than slop cows and scrape manure off his boots after all. My dream is so close. *I'm* so close.

I scan the bases one last time.

Jared Morris waits at home plate, leaning off first like he owns the whole stadium. He probably thinks he does. The moron grins like the smug jerk he is, flashing me that white smile from across the diamond. It's not like the play means anything. They're up by two runs. He's just rubbing my nose in it, staying on base to rattle me. Staying on base to piss me off, actually.

Yeah, it's working. A little bit.

"C'mon, Charlie, let's go!" Coach's voice booms out from the dugout.

I jerk my head in that direction. I've got seconds before he decides to walk me and end this. Seconds to make the pitch of a lifetime. But I know I can do it. I mean, I've done it a thousand times before, though not with my legacy on the line. So…I take one more breath and twist my shoulder into the windup. Keeping my mind blank, I let muscle memory take over. My body knows what to do.

Everyone in the crowd seems to hold their breath along with me. I push off the rubber and…Jared Morris barrels toward me like a frigging freight train. His gleeful expression distracts me at the crucial second when I let the ball fly.

Time stretches out like a bad dream that won't let me wake up, forcing me to experience every detail of Jared's obnoxious grin as he runs toward me. Then the sensation of time slowing snaps like a rubber band, and suddenly, he's so close I can see the treads on his shoes.

I can't move. It's a nightmare. A fucking nightmare.

As if it's become autonomous, my glove shoots up to stop him. But it's too late. His shoulder slams into me hard. I'm airborne for what feels like one endless moment of unbelievable shock. As I smack down on the grass with a grunt, a sharp pain knifes through every nerve in my shoulder, the pain sharp and raw. I clutch at my arm, gritting my teeth.

Something else falls onto the grass beside me. The ball. The one that was supposed to break records today. I stagger backward, dazed from the pain. Then a wave of dizziness hits me, and I nearly fall down.

Most of the crowd boos and points their fingers at Jared, but the minority gives me the full-on loser treatment. Fans of Jared Morris, obviously. They even throw food at me. I know I'm making faces like some rookie on his first day of spring training, but I can't stop it. Jesus, I can't stop it.

Then the crowd spontaneously erupts into cheers of a different kind. They shout, "Charlie! Charlie! Charlie!"

As I stagger onto the red sand of the diamond, I can't figure out what's happening. My shoulder hurts like hell, that's all I know. I squeeze my eyes shut, and I can hear my own heartbeat throbbing in my ears. Surreal spots and colors dance behind my lids like psychedelic galaxies.

Coach jogs up to me, placing a firm hand on my left arm to steady me. He's careful not to touch my right shoulder.

"I'm okay," I hear myself say. But it sounds far away and tinny, like a cheap speaker at a discount store.

"Take him into the locker room!" someone yells above the stadium noise.

That sounds like Phil Schreier. Jeez, if the team manager is here, I must be in bad shape. Several of my teammates have followed us into the locker room. I slump down onto a bench.

"Don't worry," Phil informs everyone. "We'll take care of Charlie. Right now, he needs an ice pack, so we'll start there. As for the rest of you…get back out there and win the damn game."

The crowd's gone silent. It's weird to hear total silence out there. I guess even the opposing team feels bad for me. I need to get out there and show everyone I'm okay. I'm not, but that's beside the point.

Somebody hands me a bottle of ibuprofen and a cup of water, but I don't bother to glance up. I down the pills and the water in one gulp. "I need to get back out there. Just to wave at the crowd and show them I'm not headed for the hospital."

Phil gives me a stern look, then he blows out a sigh. "Okay, Charlie."

I still feel a touch woozy, but I insist on trudging out there alone. The second I'm out of the tunnel, I raise my good arm to wave at the spectators. Cheers erupt with even more volume from everyone in the stadium. Their vocal support lifts my spirits, but I know I have a long road ahead of me before I can become the fastball hero again.

Out on the field, Jared Morris jogs by me at a discreet distance, still wearing that conceited grin. He makes a point of not looking at me.

The record-breaking pitch I'd worked so hard for slipped out of my grasp in a single moment.

Soon, the stadium disappears in the rearview mirror behind me, and I'm whisked back to my apartment with Phil as my chauffeur. I close my eyes and pretend I'm going somewhere else. A tropical beach in the South Pacific, maybe.

But nothing will ever erase the memory of what could've been but now might slip through my fingers.

All because of Jared Morris.

Chapter Two

The Ultimatum

Phil Schreier's office has the charm of a bad hospital room and none of the warmth. He sits behind his desk, all business, as my legs begin to ache in the hard-back chair. There are too many things to look at—stack of papers, an old computer, his grave expression—so I decide to stare at the floor instead.

"Here are your options," our team manager had told me two weeks ago "Improve quickly, or face a trade or demotion to the minors."

The words had hit me like a line drive. I was hoping for a pep talk, but instead, it's an execution. A snort escapes me before I can stop it. These were supposed to be my glory days. Who was I kidding? The fastball king fell from grace and couldn't crawl back up again.

"You doing okay, Charlie?" Phil's voice pulls me back to the here and now. He leans forward, hands clasped. "Tough game last night."

Understatement of the century. I nod, letting silence do the talking. My fingers drum a nervous beat on the armrest.

"The injury's healing?" he presses.

Yeah, sure, it's healing slowly—like molasses in January.

"Doc says another couple of weeks." The lie sours my tongue. A couple of weeks until what? I get another meeting like this one?

Phil tilts his head, his gaze narrowing. "You're not pitching like before, Charlie."

"I know." My fastball isn't so fast anymore, and it's all I've been thinking about. My shoulder doesn't feel that bad, but still…I can't get anywhere near Nolan Ryan's fastball and or Aroldis Chapman's. Can't even reach my own previous pitching speed. I've lost my game. For good? God, I hope not. Baseball is my life and my passion.

Phil steeples his fingers, scrutinizing me like I'm a puzzle he's trying to solve. "You understand what's at stake here, right?"

"Absolutely. I've read this chapter a hundred times. Hero falls from grace big time, keeps fucking it up over and over. No happy ending for Charlie."

He raises an eyebrow, not buying my sarcasm. "I need you to be honest. With me, with everyone. But especially with yourself."

A pause hangs in the air, the unspoken words as heavy as bricks. He's gonna send me back to the minors, isn't he?

Then Phil leans in. "Improve quickly or face a trade or demotion to the minors. Those are your choices, remember? I like you Charlie, you know that. But we can't carry a guy who's not giving us his best."

I assume I'm supposed to offer up a vow to do better or…something. But my tongue seems to have gotten stuck to the roof of my mouth. Phil waits me out, though, letting the words sink in. Letting me sink or swim, as the euphemism goes.

"I'm working on it," I assure him. What a lame excuse. "You know I've still got the fire."

Phil sighs, running a hand through his hair. "I know you think you do."

Ouch. That was a real zinger. I swear I could almost feel the pinch of those words. "I carried this team for three years, Phil, and we both know it."

His expression is one part patience, two parts pity. "No one's questioning what you've done for us. We just can't keep waiting."

And there it is. The past tense, biting into me like a rusty nail. I had a good run, but it's over. Thanks for everything, don't let the door hit your ass on the way out. I clear my throat, trying to shift the lump that's settled there.

"We're barely halfway through the season," I point out. My voice is steady, even if my gut is churning. "Things can turn around."

"If you think you can turn it around, then show us," Phil replies, his tone a shade softer but no less firm. "Soon."

What I hear is "or else." But what I feel is "how the hell will ya do that, pal?"

"I'm busting my ass every day," I insist. And I'm failing at it. "Can't believe you'd do this now."

"It's not something I want to do." Phil's eyes meet mine, and for a second, I catch a flicker of understanding in them. Then it evaporates. "You've got a month, kid."

One month? That's crazy. Maybe I should give up and start writing my memoirs—*From Hero to Zero: The Charlie Braddock Story. Available soon in hardcover and paperback.*

I heave myself up and onto my feet, feeling the world wobble a little under me. What else can I say? "Got it, boss, loud and clear."

Phil stands up too, smoothing a wrinkle from his shirt. "This isn't personal, Charlie."

It sure feels personal, for damn sure. Every game, every pitch, feels personal. I've spent too long thinking I'm the one they can't do without. Now that I'm no longer the golden boy, what should I do? Get a job holding up sandwich board signs outside a pizzeria?

I approach the door, my fingers clutching the handle like it's a lifeline. "I'll get it together, Phil, I promise."

"We'll be watching." He sounds like a coach. But he means it like a judge.

I slam the door behind me and storm down the hallway. The sound reverberates through the corridor, but my anger echoes even louder inside me. My footsteps pound the linoleum, echoing like they're trying to outrun me. I wish I could outrun myself. The hallway is narrow, cold, and I feel its chill down to my bones. Phil's words burn in my ears.

I don't remember much after leaving the office. It's like there's a bell going off inside my head, telling me I've got one month, one month, one month. It won't stop ringing, won't let me think about anything else. I want to punch something, someone, anyone. A stack of boxes in the hallway gets the side-eye, but they don't deserve it. Not like I do.

How did I not see Jared coming at me sooner? If I'd paid better attention, maybe I wouldn't be in this mess—on the verge of becoming a has-been, a sad footnote in the annals of baseball history.

I pause halfway down the hall, head bowed, hands on my hips. Phil's ultimatum echoes in my mind. But it feels more like a death sentence than a second chance. The words replay in my head, ugly and real. Improve quickly, Charlie. Because we're all waiting around for you, Charlie. And you can't stop being a failure, Charlie.

I thought this was my year to crush the World Series. I thought I was on top again. What a joke. Thinking is clearly not my strong suit these days.

The fluorescent lights buzz above me, casting a eerie glow on everything, including my pathetic attempt to play it cool back there. I hate how the walls are so sterile, the way they make me feel like a specimen under a microscope. An experiment gone wrong. I pick up the pace, trying to get away from myself. No surprise that I'm the only one chasing me.

Phil admonished me not to take it personally. But my career, all the years I'd busted my ass for the team, it's as personal as it gets. Every step I take echoes back at me, sounding like the hollow truth I didn't want to hear.

A murmur catches my ear, stopping me in my tracks. That's Phil's voice. I recognize it before I realize where it's coming from. An open door, just a crack. Curiosity wins, not like it's a competition. I pause, holding my breath.

"…can't afford to wait. Need him to turn around fast." His voice is neutral, like this is just business. "Thinking of hiring a new trainer for him. Exclusive."

The words hit me like cold water doused over my head. I'm frozen to this spot, trapped between staying to eavesdrop and sprinting away. Is that what they really think of me? That I can't even fix myself without a babysitter? Nice to know their faith is as strong as my batting average.

My fists clench at my sides, tight enough to hurt. Phil is still talking, but I can't hear what he's saying anymore. I don't want to hear it. It's one more reminder that I'm a walking cautionary tale about faded glory. Maybe the trainer can help with that too.

I push my hands through my hair. Now, even if I claw my way back to the top, everyone will still remember me as the pitcher whose shoulder got fucked, and he left his team hanging in mid-season.

Leaning against the wall, I feel its cold bite through my shirt. My bag slips off my shoulder and hits the floor with a thud. I want to scream. I want to laugh. But I do neither. Instead, I simply stand here with my eyes burning and my heart beating out the countdown. I have one month, one new trainer, and no chance in hell.

The burn in my eyes…no, I am not about to cry. Wouldn't that be pathetic? It's dust, that's all.

I pick up my bag and take one last look at the open door and what's left of my pride. Doesn't that go before a fall? Jeez, even the bible wants to dunk on me. What else can I do? I walk away from the conversation, from the office, from myself. My footsteps echo again, but they sound different now.

Goodbye, fastball king. Hello, starting over.

I just pray my new trainer is a badass with five tattoos and biceps like a gorilla. Only someone like that might have a chance of saving my career.

Chapter Three

Enter the Coach

The interior of the training facility feels like a jail cell, not that I've ever been in jail. But this little corner of the hallway I've been relegated to feels almost as confining. It's like I've been punished with a timeout in kindergarten, only worse. I've lost my edge. Why? Because I worry my shoulder will never heal. I deserve whatever punishment Phil has decided to heap on me.

I drum my fingers on my knees while I wait for my sentence to be handed down. This crappy chair makes my ass hurt, and I swear somebody put needles in the padding. The murmur of conversation filters out of Phil's office, too quiet for me to understand the words. The door hangs half-open in a taunting invitation I don't dare accept.

"Charlie's recovery isn't just about his future," I hear Phil say. Every syllable feels like a gut punch. "It's the team's World Series dream, not just one pitcher's."

Whoever he's talking to, I still can't make out their words.

Speak up, would ya? Don't leave me hanging.

They shuffle around inside the office as if they've made their decision and informing me is an afterthought. I'm already out of the game. Because of my injury. My dreams don't mean shit anymore.

The quiet outside the office begins to feel suffocating, and I push up out of my chair. While I shuffle my feet on the concrete floor, I'm unsure whether I should stay and hear the truth or walk away and pretend I didn't. The door remains open as if it's daring me to make a decision.

I lean against the wall but can't stop tapping my foot.

A piece of loose thread on my shirt catches my attention, and I yank at it, unraveling more than I intended. It hangs there, like a visible reminder of everything else in my life that's coming apart. I can't let the team down, can't let myself become the guy who once had potential.

My skin itches, and I struggle against scratching.

"We need to do everything to help him recover—and not just physically."

That voice—a woman's voice—resounds clearly and firmly.

I slide closer to the doorway but still out of sight, straining to catch the rest of what's being said.

"Mentally too," the mystery woman declares.

Does she think I'm unbalanced or something? That's crap. Who is that woman, anyway?

The door swings open all the way, and Phil steps out, as calm as ever. "Charlie, come on in."

I freeze briefly before trailing him into the office. My heart thumps hard against my ribcage like it's trying to break free. Phil motions for me to sit while I size up his company. There she is—athletic build, chestnut hair tied back, hazel eyes sharp and almost…challenging.

"This is Amy Keller," Phil explains. "She'll be your new coach."

Whuh, what? I think my head might be smoking, like a cartoon character. Phil couldn't have said this woman is…my coach? The word slams into me with the force of a fastball. Maybe Phil gave me a pretty new coach with mesmerizing eyes as a test of some sort.

Amy Keller gives me half a smile, the kind that suggests she means business more than friendship. "Nice to meet you, Charlie."

Yeah, great, whatever. I slump down onto the chair, still reeling from what Phil's just told me. "You're kidding, right? About the coach thing?"

The words tumble out before I can stop myself. *Smart move, Braddock.*

Despite the tension in the room, Amy doesn't flinch. Her gaze bores into mine with unflappable determination. "No joke, Braddock. I've taken on bigger challenges than you."

I glance over at Phil, searching for a sign that Amy Keller's appearance is nothing more than a way to screw with my head. Phil's as steady as ever.

"The team needs you back in top form," Phil asserts. "Amy's got the experience to help you get there."

My thoughts scramble like eggs in a pan. A woman coach? How's that gonna fly with the rest of the guys? I open my mouth to argue, but Amy cuts me off.

"Don't worry about your teammates and what they might think of your situation," she explains, as if she's read my mind. "Your comeback is priority one. But if you can't hack the long hours of training, tell me now. You aren't so special that we can't bear to trade you."

Damn, she's tough—and she doesn't even blink when she says things like that. Her words bite, and I can feel their sting long after she's done.

"So, what's the plan, then?" I'm trying to sound more in control than I feel. This is my career, after all, and nobody else can save it for me.

Amy leans back in her chair, arms crossed. "We start tomorrow. Bright and early. Hope you like running at sunup, Braddock."

Sounds like the seventh circle of hell to me. But if I want back in the game—if I want to keep my place on the team—I need to show her she can't scare me away.

I straighten up and stare directly into her eyes. "Fine. See you then, Coach."

Phil pats me on the shoulder as I stand, his touch almost reassuring. Almost. Amy just nods, a silent acknowledgment that feels more like a challenge than anything else. I'm not used to dealing with women like her. Women who look hardball in the eye and don't blink. I'm almost impressed—but not quite. I can feel the intensity rolling off her, and I'm not sure if it charges me up or cuts me down.

Phil claps a hand on my shoulder, squeezing hard, though not enough to cause pain. "You two will be spending a lot of time together over the next few months."

Amy lifts her brows. "Not if he keeps stalling."

Now she's got me cornered. It's a crafty tactic. I recognize it from facing every smartass batter who ever thought they had my number. Pressure me until I crack or rise to the challenge. I force myself to sit even more upright, ignoring the pain that shoots through my shoulder like someone's jabbing it with a hot poker.

"I'm not stalling," I squeeze out between gritted teeth.

Her half-smile returns, the one that suggests she doesn't believe a word of anything I've said. Phil waves us off with an easygoing grin. Amy's already ahead of me, her strides quick and confident as we leave the office.

"Good luck, Charlie," Phil calls after me, which is either encouragement or a farewell before my execution. Not sure which is the worse option.

The air outside the office feels like the sweetest, cleanest oxygen after an undersea dive to the bottom of the ocean. I can breathe again, only now every breath reminds me of what tomorrow holds. Amy walks briskly just ahead of me, not bothering to check if I'm keeping up. She expects me to trail after her, I'm sure, like some rookie who got called up too soon.

I trot to catch up with her, desperate to regain some ground. "Do you always assume your players will crumble like cookies?"

She doesn't even glance back. "Only when they act like they might."

Great, now I'm hungry for chocolate chip cookies. I manage to stay by her side as she pushes open the doors to the parking lot, the sun hitting us like a stadium spotlight. "You do realize you've got your work cut out for you, right? I'm not exactly known for going easy—on coaches or myself."

She lifts her chin, those beautiful hazel eyes sparkling with a challenge aimed directly at me. "I never said I wanted it easy, Braddock. Let's see what you've got."

With that, she heads toward her car, leaving me standing here more riled up than ever—and more confused than ever too. I watch her driving away and wonder how someone so sure of herself could knock me off balance when I barely know her. This is going to be one hell of a fight, and it's too late to pretend I'm not ready to swing with everything I've got.

My shoulder protests as I shuffle up to my car. Tomorrow looms in my head like a mountain I'm expected to sprint up before breakfast. But fear and adrenaline knot together inside me, pushing back against the doubt I couldn't shake this morning. Working with Amy will be rough. Maybe impossible. But even if she's a hard-nosed ball-buster, I can handle it. I have three sisters, after all.

Amy's taillights disappear as she peels out of the parking lot, leaving me to stew in the heat and my own second thoughts. I crank the engine and lean my head back for a few minutes to ensure I won't crash my car because I'm still fuming over Amy's comments about me.

A figure dashes up to the driver's side window. I glance up and groan.

Jared Morris knocks on the glass and keeps knocking until I give up and roll down the window. "What do you want, Morris?"

"Heard you got a girl for a coach. That sucks. Wittle Chucky needs a bwankie to cry on, huh?"

"Go suck a lemon, jackass."

Jared grins and chuckles.

I roll up the window and ram my foot down on the gas pedal, swerving out of my parking slot backwards, just barely missing another car. In the rearview mirror, I see Jared still grinning. Somehow, I manage to get home without killing myself or anyone else. By the time I tumble into bed, only a sliver of light hovers on the horizon, about to vanish. I try not to think about how soon I'll be hearing my alarm clock or how much I'd rather just turn it all off and let sleep swallow me whole.

If Amy Keller thinks she can lob an underarm throw at me, she's got another thing coming. My lids shut on that thought while exhaustion wipes my brain clean for a few blessed hours.

Chapter Four

Reluctant Partnership

The training room's a wreck—bats, helmets, and gear flung everywhere. My foot connects with a baseball and sends it skittering across the floor. It's like walking through a damn minefield. I hate this place, the low drone of the lights, the smell of sweat and desperation. It's the smell of failure, I guess, and it's wafting off me in waves. My shoulder feels stiff, and I rotate it, hoping nobody's around to see me wince.

To escape the stale smells, I head outside.

That's when I notice her, standing by the pitching mound like she's the new fastball queen who'll take over my slot on the team. Amy holds a clipboard in one hand, and her ponytail bobs as she shakes her head slightly. Amy wears an Admirals cap, and she's waiting for me. Her confident stance and expression make me uneasy.

"What took you so long, Braddock?" she asks. "Must've been playing with your ball for too long this morning."

Maybe I am holding a shiny new ball in my hand, but I don't appreciate her innuendo. Wouldn't mind feeling up those luscious tits, though. Or her lips, which she's currently licking over and over like she wants to devour me.

Amy glances down at the bulge in my pants, her lips curling up at one corner in an appreciative way. Then she makes a come-hither gesture. It doesn't seem sexual at all, unfortunately. That's just the way a coach might summon a player. I halt an arm's length from her.

My coach shakes her head and frowns slightly. "Did you go on a bender last night? You look like hell, Braddock."

"Why are you riding my ass so hard? This is how I am first thing in the morning, buttercup. Impressed yet?"

She ignores the dig and checks something off her clipboard, completely unfazed. "You need rehab, not a babysitter. You'll hate me most of the time, but I'm the only one who can turn you around and keep you out of the minors."

I snort. "You talk tough, but let's see your credentials, sweetheart. I bet you're fresh off the T-ball circuit."

"Let's see your World Series ring, sweetheart," she fires back, and damn if it doesn't sting more than I want to admit.

I drop the ball and fold my arms over my chest. "Guess you're also the new team shrink, huh?"

"Coach, Braddock, not shrink." Her steely gaze locks onto mine. Those eyes are fierce, daring me to keep making excuses. "Are you ready to get to work yet? Or would you rather whine and moan some more?"

Wouldn't mind making her moan…but that would get me into way more trouble. "I'm here, aren't I? That's proof I want to do the work."

Amy puckers her lips and squints at me for long enough that I start to get seriously annoyed. But I take a deep breath and release all the tension. Well, as much as I reasonably can, considering the circumstances. I glance around at the weights and resistance bands scattered at her feet like some medieval torture setup.

My coach sets down the clipboard and steps up to me with confidence in her stance and her eyes. "Let's start with some basics. Show me those stretches we talked about."

"Here? On the field?"

She rolls her eyes. "No, Braddock. You'll train in the workout room until I decide you're ready for more. Let's go."

Amy walks away without another word, and I follow like a scolded puppy. Everything inside me screams to fight back, but there's something about her that makes resistance feel futile. Nothing special about the workout room either, with its cold floors and mirrors that force you to face reality. I was hoping for a miracle, but it's the same as always—a place where players go to work off their frustrations or work through their loser phases.

Amy picks up a resistance band, tossing it at me. "Let's see what you've got, hotshot."

I catch the band just in time, fumbling only a little. "You mean I have to do all the work myself?"

She laughs, which throws me off guard because it sounds melodic, like she really finds me funny instead of just pathetic. "Afraid of a little exercise? I thought you'd be happy I wasn't hovering over you."

Her words needle at me until all my thoughts blur into one persistent hum: Prove her wrong. I loop the band around the bar and give it a test pull. My shoulder complains, but I grit my teeth and keep going.

"That the best you can muster?" Amy isn't even writing anything down. She simply stands there, hands on her hips, like she's waiting for me to collapse into a puddle and burst into tears. "This is me taking it easy. Can't risk showing off too much at the start."

"Uh-huh. Try lowering your shoulder a bit."

I do it her way, fighting the urge to tell her where she can stick that pointer finger of hers. "Like this?"

"Exactly like that." She smiles, and I wonder if she's surprised that I listened—and did what she wanted me to do.

I push through a couple more reps, each one loosening the stiffness in my shoulder and winding it tighter in my chest. "What's next, boss?"

"Weights. But with the way you're huffing and puffing already…"

A quick glance over my shoulder tells me she's serious, and I don't know whether to be impressed or frustrated. I drop the band and move to the weights. "You trying to kill me, Coach?"

Her lips quirk into an almost smirk. "Just waking you up."

Oh, trust me, baby, I'm awake. Your sexy body keeps me charged up all day and all night, if only in my dreams.

Amy hands me a dumbbell. Her fingers brush against mine, and my dick twitches, though she doesn't seem to notice. "A light one for your delicate condition, old man."

"Gonna give me one in pink?"

"Would you prefer sparkles?" She lifts her chin, and there's a dare in her eyes.

I grunt and get started. The reps go smoother than I expect, but by the last set I'm ready to call it a day and possibly a career. Still, there's something satisfying about it too—like proving her wrong is more important than anything else. The burn in my muscles distracts me from the gnawing doubt in my head. I set the weight down with a clatter and a pointed look at her, waiting for more smart remarks.

She doesn't take my bait. Instead, she nods and scribbles something on that damn clipboard of hers. "So, what do you think, Braddock? Ready to trade me for someone with bigger tits?"

The question knocks the wind out of me. Is my coach hitting on me? That would be sexual harassment. So I must have misheard her. I pull in a sharp breath before answering. "I'll give you two more sessions. If I'm not seeing results by then…"

Amy raises an eyebrow, waiting for me to finish my thought. Waiting for me to crack.

"If I'm not seeing results, you're fired—and so am I."

She smiles with satisfaction as if she expected nothing less from me. "Good. Make a decision about your wife before then too."

Her eyes flick down to my left hand.

I stopped wearing my ring the day after my ex-wife filed for divorce and announced she was going back to her maiden name. "Alicia is my ex-wife. I rarely see her these days, and I'm not in love with her anymore."

"Glad to hear it."

"You don't need to worry about my love life interfering with recovery. I haven't even dated anyone casually for at least a year."

"Good." Amy folds her arms and squints at me. "If there's one thing worse than a has-been, it's a has-been with girl problems." She waves toward the door. "Now get out of here. Show up tomorrow ready to work even harder."

I flash her a cocky smile, but my heart's not really in it. "You mean ready to whine and bitch?"

"Love that enthusiasm," Amy says with a smirk as she turns away, leaving me with nothing but the cold workout room and my own lousy thoughts.

What she doesn't understand is how desperate I am—desperate enough to beg for help before I leap off the side of the Titanic. But she'll figure it out. One thing I've learned is that Amy Keller is whip smart. Two more sessions? Hell, she'll have me figured out by lunch tomorrow.

I leave the training room, feeling like I've been run over by a truck and then kicked by a mule for good measure. It's a good kind of whipped, though.

Outside, the sun beats down so hot that I start to wonder if my car will melt into a puddle on the asphalt, and I squint into the bright Jacksonville morning. Well, late morning. My body might be spent, but my mind is on overdrive. Maybe I should've mentioned to Amy that my ex-wife popped up again last week and rattled my cage with a sexy offer for tequila shots that we would drink off each other's bodies. The offer was tempting, but…

I'd rather fuck Amy.

Oh, no you don't, moron. Coach Keller is the only one who can get you into shape, so don't screw it up.

No sex for Charlie. Damn.

I settle for a slice of celibacy pie and make my way to the locker room, hoping a shower might rinse off at least some of this defeat. The room's empty, except for a couple pairs of beat-up cleats sitting in the corner like they're taunting me. I fumble with my locker and dig out a towel.

Water beats down on my back, almost too hot but not quite enough to scald out the mess in my head. Amy's voice echoes in my mind—has-been, girl troubles, old man. Everything I already know but don't want to hear. I soap up and try to focus on the fact that I survived day one without falling apart. That's gotta count for something.

Hopefully, humiliation burns calories.

Just as I'm about to step out of the shower, my mind decides to torture me with images of Amy's hot body. Those luscious tits. Her toned muscles. The way her stiff nipples jutted. I feel too wired to go home, but I need to rest my muscles. When I glance down, I suddenly realize why I'm wired.

My dick is waving like a flag.

Aw, shit. How long will it take for my cock to go flaccid? Yeah, those are words I never imagined I'd think. The face of my sexy coach flashes through my mind, and suddenly, I'm breathing harder. Only one way to cure this little, ah, problem.

I wrap my hand around my cock and begin to pump in a rhythm that feels like an intimate dance, a solo performance where every stroke brings me closer to the edge—with Amy's face hovering in front of me. Here, I am the master of this dirty workout, every movement deliberate and familiar, promising satisfaction. The wet sound of my hand pumping fills the space, along with my grunts and hissing breaths.

"Fuck," I growl. "Amy, ah…"

I hiss and snarl, pumping faster and more urgently while I slap a palm flat on the shower wall. I pump until my legs quiver and a surge of molten pleasure floods through me. Oh, shit. I rest my head against the tile, letting the steam envelop me as I wait for my pulse to slow its wild pace. How long has it been since I indulged myself like this in the shower? It feels like an eternity. I never came this hard in the shower when I was married to Alicia.

Amy Keller turns me into a maniac.

When I finally drag myself out of the shower and get dressed, the locker room is still empty. Just me and some chipped linoleum tiles as an audience. Clean and dressed, I check my phone. Four messages from Alicia. Can't resist smiling even though I should know better.

Alicia: *Dinner tonight? Pick you up after training?*

Charlie: *Sorry, busy tonight.*

Before my ex-wife can try to seduce me into falling back into old habits, I shove my phone into my hip pocket. The parking lot's mostly empty, just a few cars are still here. Mine sits under a tree, and I'm grateful for the shade. I slide into the driver's seat gingerly, feeling my morning workout throbbing in every muscle. My phone buzzes again the moment I sit down. I can guess who it is. It would be damn nuts to look.

So, of course, I do.

Alicia: *Brunch tomorrow? You can't resist mimosas with me.*

I let that statement hang in the air as I fire up the engine, blasting sports radio as if that will shake off the living ghost of my failed marriage. A panel of analysts speculate about trades and line-ups, the Admirals' chances of making the playoffs this season, and more. They talk about me like I'm already gone—"the player formerly known as Charlie"—and I twist the dial to shut them up mid-sentence.

Back at my apartment, I kick off my shoes and sprawl out on the sofa, too wiped to crawl into the bedroom. I live alone, so who cares if I don't even bother taking my shirt off.

If Amy doesn't kill me tomorrow, Alicia just might.

Chapter Five

Wisdom from the Dugout

My muscles burn. I can feel every step like a needle in my knee as I trudge into the dugout, leaving another brutal practice behind. Amy's methods are ruthless. She stands on the field with her arms crossed, barking orders at me or whoever else gets in the way of the routine she's mapped out for me—or should I say the torture she's mapped out. I collapse onto the bench, ignoring the way it groans under my weight, and stare out at the Jacksonville skyline glowing in the distance.

It's almost dark, but she's still out there.

My teammates gave up on practicing a while ago. As they left the field, the guys gave me encouraging thumbs-ups as well as grins and winks. Yeah, they've supported me all the way. But I have a feeling that if I can't get my fastball back soon, I'll be a former member of the Jacksonville Admirals.

Now that Amy and I are alone, I can't help but notice the way she stretches her arms above her head. The movement awakens my dick in a way I really don't want to happen right now. I swerve my head in the opposite direction, but my eyes insist on following her. Phil is already here in the dugout, shuffling through papers like he doesn't have a care in the world.

"Long day?" he asks, raising his head just enough to glance at me sideways.

"Yeah, it feels that way," I mutter. My shirt clings to my skin, and even I can smell the sweaty stench wafting off me.

Phil goes back to his paperwork.

And I...well, I can't stop my mind from reliving every movement Amy made during our session. The way her tits bounce when she pretends to throw a pitch. How she bites her lip with her tongue sticking out a little every time she does that. Oh, and I can't forget how she wriggles her ass while playing the umpire to my pitcher.

Yet I also can't forget the training routine. It's indelibly inked on my brain.

Amy's voice still echoes in my ears too, compelling me to remember how she pushed me to my limits, demanding more, unrelenting in her determination. That's exactly what a great coach ought to do. She's driven me into the ground since day one, and I'm beginning to realize that's what I've needed all along. Her whip-cracking is the only thing that might get me back to where I was before the injury. But every time I see her, every time I hear her call my name, the most inappropriate thoughts fill my head.

"You did well out there," Phil says. "Amy's a ballbuster, but she knows what she's doing."

I nod absently. Maybe I should give her credit, but I'm still pissed that I even care what she thinks of me.

The stadium is mostly empty, the distant sound of cars drifting in from outside. The metal bench is cold beneath me. It's peaceful in a way, and I let myself relax for the first time all day. I watch Phil, his sturdy frame leaning over the clipboard, his pen scratching methodically against the paper.

"You know," he says without looking up, "you are getting your form back."

"Doesn't feel like it." I flex my fingers, feeling the dull throb that races all the way up my arm. Still, I can't deny the pain has been lessening lately.

"It will come back," Phil assures me, his tone calm with a confident ring to it, like he's said these words a hundred times and they've always come true. "You'll be the fastball king again, trust me."

"Does Amy ever quit?" I ask, more to myself than to Phil.

He chuckles. "Not likely."

My gaze flicks to Amy, who's talking to another coach, and they both laugh at something one or the other said. Whenever Amy smiles...damn, it's hot. Makes me want to drag her into the nearest secluded spot and kiss her until she melts into me.

Phil turns toward me. "Ya know, I've watched you two out there. You and Amy."

I stiffen, confused about where he's going with this. "And?"

"Reminds me of when I was still playing."

I look at him, really look at him, and it's easy to forget sometimes that Phil was in my shoes once. His beard is starting to gray, and there's wisdom in his eyes that feels earned.

But I haven't earned anything yet. "What about me and Amy reminds you of your glory days?"

"Pushing too hard, getting frustrated, feeling like it's all slipping away. And someone standing there, making sure it didn't."

I follow his gaze back to Amy. She's ambling toward us both, though I'm sure she's aiming for me. I haven't been fully whipped yet today, after all. Not that I mind those whippings all that much these days.

Phil shifts on the bench, and I hear the soft rustle of paper. "You know how I ended up here?"

I shake my head, curious despite myself.

"I was the next big thing. Power hitter, tons of speed." He smiles as if he doesn't quite believe it anymore himself. "Then one game, I take a pitch right to the wrist. Bone shatters. Just like that, I'm off the roster. Not much to do when you're sitting on the sidelines and everyone's moving on without you."

His words hit me harder than any fastball. I don't interrupt, letting him continue.

"The manager told me I was washed up. Offered me a coaching job in Single-A. Might as well have been the bottom of the ocean. But I took it. Couldn't imagine not being in the game at all." He pauses, his gaze catching mine. "I spent years building myself back, little by little. Worked my way up to manager. I learned the hard way that it takes more than muscle to get back in the game."

I exhale a slow, shaky breath. His story hangs in the air between us, heavy and real. "And your wrist?"

"Doing just fine. But not major league fine. Doesn't matter anymore, though, because I love being team manager."

I lean back, feeling the cool wood press against my back, and wonder if he's gently prepping me for the possibility that I won't get my game back. But I shouldn't think that way. I won't think that way.

Phil picks up the papers, stacking them with practiced ease. I watch him, absorbing the steady, comforting presence that he brings to this team. "Don't lose heart, Charlie. It's a process, and you're not alone."

Maybe I do have something left, and I just need to believe it.

Phil stands up, tucking the papers under his arm. "I'll see you tomorrow, Charlie."

I manage only a tight smile.

While Phil walks away, the clinking of his pen fades, leaving me alone with my thoughts.

Amy finally reaches the dugout, though she lingers on the top step, her hands grasping the roof. "Time to go home, Charlie. You need rest before our next session."

"Yes, ma'am."

I uncoil my body, wincing at the protest in my muscles, and stretch out the stiffness. As I grab my gear, I turn away from Amy in the process. When I shuffle around to face her, I'm stunned to realize she's moved directly in front of me. I stare at her blankly, unable to move even one millimeter. Her hot breaths tickle my face.

"Everything okay, Amy?"

She nods slowly, biting her lip, releasing it little by little until it springs free. Her gaze wanders over my entire body. Why she wants to smell the stench of my sweat is beyond me.

"Amy?" I ask, feeling weird about this encounter.

She grasps a handful of my shirt, dragging me closer. "I have a radical idea for speeding up your recovery."

"No electric shock, please. My brain's already fried enough right now."

Amy ignores my dumb joke and instead stares deeply into my eyes. Her voice has grown huskier. "Do you trust me, Charlie?"

"Yeah, of course. You are my coach, after all." And I'm getting turned on more and more by the second, making my chest rise and fall with every breath.

She grazes her fingers over my cheek. "I don't usually like stubbly men, but your shadow beard makes me so damn hot for you."

My entire body freezes, from my toes all the way up to my scalp. It's a sexy kind of frozen, though. The sort that makes my dick spring to attention.

Amy licks her lips unhurriedly, dragging them back and forth. My breathing grows ragged and heavier. Her voice is throatier now when she finally speaks. "I believe the only thing that will supercharge your recovery is…sex."

Her words fire an electric jolt straight through me, like I've taken a hundred-mile-an-hour fastball straight to the chest—but in a good way. A really good way. She's tugging on my shirt, and the tug travels downward gradually until she reaches the hard-on straining against my pants.

"Is this some kind of cruel experiment?" I can barely breathe or speak. Though I try to sound cool, there's too much hoarseness in my voice to pull it off.

Amy leans into me, her gaze intense. "This is no experiment, Charlie."

Only now have I noticed she's calling me Charlie instead of Braddock.

That does it. Every molecule in my body leaps for her all at once. I close the gap between us at lightning speed. But then I slow down, brushing my lips against hers so tentatively that I might as well be a twelve-year-old who's experienced his first crush on the cutest girl in school.

Amy doesn't want to wait for me to unfreeze. She kisses me harder than I expect—than anyone should ever expect. And holy fuck, it feels amazing.

Chapter Six

Simmering Chemistry

Amy moans when I wrap my arms around her and thrust my tongue between her lips. She slings her arms around my neck, sinking her fingers deep into my hair. The feel of her lips crushed to mine, the flavor of her kisses, it all drives me out of my mind with a lust I can't contain. Never in my life have I wanted a woman so desperately. Her bossiness and determination make me so damn hot for her.

I'm about to strip her shirt off over her head and take what I've wanted since the moment we met…when she shuffles away from me, pulling out of my arms. Her lips are a deep pink, and they're swollen too. As for me, I can barely catch my breath.

She gives me a playful, taunting grin like nothing I've seen from her before. "Break's over, Braddock."

Amy whirls around, stalking out of the dugout.

Christ. This woman is going to kill me. I stand here, wobbly on my feet, while I try to figure out what just happened. The most amazing kiss ever, that's what. But I'm still sizzling from that kiss, which means I need to wait until my blossoming erection softens enough that I won't scare anyone. Once I've reached that point, I drive home and hit the sack.

Yeah, sure, I slept okay last night. If tossing and turning counts as restful.

This morning, the field is blazing hot for morning practice with heat already shimmering off the bases. I take my cap off, waving it in my face in an attempt to cool down. Amy is relentless with the entire squad today. Phil wants us ready for Morris and the Assitudes next week—the first game in a grueling road stretch—so Amy pushes us through extra rounds of hitting and fielding practice. She barely gets off the diamond to eat lunch with me.

Okay, the Assitudes isn't the official name for our nemesis team. The real name is too pathetic to speak aloud—Aspen Altitude. Yeah, those jerks think apres-ski is a sport of its own.

"How's your arm?" Amy casually asks while I shovel half my sandwich into my mouth in one bite.

"Good," I mumble around chunks of bread and turkey. "Only the occasional mini-twinge."

She doesn't let me slide with that answer for a second. "Can you throw tomorrow or not? The truth, not quips."

I give a single nod and a thumbs-up, my mouth too full to respond.

"Good." She folds her arms over her chest. "Double drills tomorrow morning, then."

I choke a little in mid-swallow. "Double?"

A sly smile spreads across her lips. "Hmm, sounds like someone needs to work on his endurance."

She's teasing me again—the same kind of grin that had me craving her like mad yesterday. The woman knows exactly what she's doing to me. I might hate it if it wasn't so fucking sexy.

As we finish lunch, the rest of the squad filters out of the clubhouse, stretching and yawning as they take their places on the field. Amy is already in the dugout, clipboard in hand, barking orders before I can get another word in.

"Let's go!" she hollers. "Grab your gloves! Move!"

Her voice reverberates across the diamond, and players scramble to line up.

By now, my arm is definitely sore, but I won't tell Amy that. Not after pretending the pain was nothing and getting double drills to celebrate my supposed recovery. I dive into practice with every bit of energy I have left. We put in another few hours before she finally calls it a day and cracks a joke about me limping back to my car. I never limp, and she knows it. It's my frigging shoulder that bothers me. But it is better than it was a few days ago.

Amy must know I'm exhausted—I can hardly stand up straight—but something tells me she won't let me get away with admitting it and begging off tomorrow's drills.

Gray clouds gather overhead while the whole team jogs out of the training ground. I can smell rain in the air, heavy and humid. By the time I get home, all I want to do is rinse off the sweat and crash in bed.

Fresh out of the shower, I slump on my couch with an ice pack on my shoulder. Sleep is next on my list, but then my phone rings.

Morris's obnoxious mug flashes across the screen and some part of me is tempted—just for a second—to toss it across the room and pretend I didn't notice the call. Why on earth did I ever give him my number? Because when I first met Jared, he'd been friendly. Then I found out he loves to troll everybody on my team.

Rather than swiping left, I answer with a curt, "What'd ya want, dipstick?"

"Hey, Braddock! Make sure you bring your smokin' coach," Jared says, sniggering. I can almost hear him grinning through the phone. "I'd hate for the Altitude to trample you too hard."

"Worry about your own team, Morris."

His cackling laughter is loud and abrasive. "You're still playing with a wet-noodle arm, huh? Last I heard, you were barely handling practice."

"You must be talking about someone else." I try to keep my voice steady and cool. He's trolling me again, since nobody on the Admirals team would leak any details of my injury.

"We'll see about that, Chucky." Jared pauses, just long enough for him to make me think it's over. And he's just dumb enough to think that'll work. "Tell your new Playboy centerfold coach not to wear you out too much. Save a little something for me."

I clench my jaw. And I think smoke might be coming out of my ears.

The line clicks off before I can respond. *That bastard.*

I slump back into the couch and try not to let Jared's taunts get to me. It doesn't matter what he says. I'll be waiting to punch him in the jaw. For now, I turn my thoughts away from him and toss my phone aside. I do my best to ignore every loudmouthed word Morris said. It's not hard, because Amy replaces them in an instant. Her voice, her eyes…her soft, yielding lips.

Rested or not, I'm first at the practice field in the morning, shoulder iced and taped. Once I'm ready, I head out to the diamond. And damn if Amy doesn't have me doing insane drills from the get-go. I love the way she looks during lap five—tight braid coming loose as she bounds after me armed with a whistle and stopwatch. This is Amy Keller at her most intense, but I can't help wondering if there's more passion where last night's kiss came from.

Jared doesn't have a clue how wrong he is—I'm more ready than ever to put him back in his place tomorrow.

"Pick it up!" Amy's voice booms across the field. She points at her watch without stopping or even slowing down half a step.

I'm running sprints side by side with Ron Peeters when the rain finally bursts from the clouds to drench us all in an instant. I glance up, wiping my eyes. This is a frigging deluge.

Amy doesn't seem to notice or care that we're soaking wet. "This is nothing! Keep it going!"

Ron and a couple other guys groan like they're about to go on strike, but they keep sprinting in spite of it. Lightning crackles in the distance, and Amy reluctantly calls it a day just before the deluge turns into Noah's flood. It's still coming down in buckets as players scatter to their cars.

Once everyone else has peeled out of the lot, I take my time getting out of my soaked shirt. On days like this, having a spare is the only thing that will stave off a cold. I'm about to leave when I see Amy get out of her car and trudge back toward me, her head down as the rain pummels her, plastering her hair to her face.

The nearest shelter is in the dugout. So, I rush to Amy and grab her hand as we race back to the dugout.

"Stupid piece of shit car wouldn't start," she half-shouts over the downpour.

I fumble with the hoodie in my hand and toss it over her. "Here."

She stares at me, blinking rapidly. "You're giving me your sweatshirt now?"

"You're soaked. Might catch cold." I struggle to stop myself from staring at her nipples that are visible thanks to her wet shirt. "Never seen you back down because of a little weather."

She grabs the dry shirt and pulls it tightly around her shoulders. "Even I have limits."

Raindrops stream down my face as we move closer to one another. The dugout roof keeps the worst of the downpour at bay, but it's still louder than a drum line in here. Both of us are short of breath, and our steamy breaths fill the air.

I squeeze water out of my hair. "Is this how you planned to get me alone, Coach?"

Amy laughs. "You caught me. A dead battery is the oldest trick in the book."

"And you didn't think I'd leave you stranded?"

"Not for one second."

Her grin makes my heart beat faster. "So…you outlasted most of the Admirals today."

"Yep, I did." She arches an eyebrow. "But not you."

I note the challenge in her voice—hell, I've been noticing it since before I kissed her. We're inches apart now, so close that I feel it more than see it when she shivers beneath that sweatshirt. I press my lips to hers, my voice lowering to a deeper, rougher register. "Let's warm ourselves up the organic way—with one mind-blowing fuck."

Amy grins.

Chapter Seven

Getting Down and Dirty

I drag her down onto my lap, the wooden bench providing a solid backdrop and plenty of room for Amy to spread her thighs over my lap. The scent of her arousal permeates the space, proof of how badly she wants me. It's the most enticing aroma I've ever experienced. Sure, I've had sex with my fair share of women—though never any groupies—but none of them got me as worked up as Amy Keller does.

I'm hard as a rock, but I want to take my time with this woman. I trail my fingers up her neck and lace them in her hair, pulling her down for a deep, searing kiss. She draws back right when I'm getting into it, her gaze cautious as she searches my eyes.

"What if somebody sees us?" she asks breathily.

"Like who? Everybody's gone home."

I peel the wet clothes off her body, piece by piece, dropping them onto the ground. Every splat indicates another garment has fallen and I'm another minute closer to making her scream. Amy pulls her bra off herself, now gloriously nude and aroused, her chest dappled with the rosy color of lust.

"No panties?" I ask. "How naughty, Coach Keller. I love that."

She helps pull my T-shirt over my head, then tugs it off. She unzips my pants, but I swat her hands away and rip my pants off. I'm desperate to feel her skin against mine, and the scent of her hunger for me grows headier and stronger by the second. My dick is stiff and waving like a flag, as if it's saying, "Come and fuck me, Amy." Even the yellowish glow of the light above us can't diminish her beauty. Amy's nipples feel as firm as pearls when I flick my thumbs over them. My mouth waters at the sight of her naked body, but I won't touch her yet. I let her catch me looking. Whatever she sees in my eyes, she clearly likes it.

The first time our naked bodies collide, I groan deep in my throat. Her tight abs move against me as she rocks closer, and the motion is pure heaven—and hell, because if she keeps this up, all my plans to go nice and slow will be shot to pieces.

I grip her waist, holding her still for a moment while I try to get hold of myself, sucking in ragged breaths that smell like rain and Amy's cream. She shivers faintly, maybe from the cold air on her hot skin, but also from the desire that's taken hold of us both. Her head falls back as I stroke the firm bud of her clit with two fingers and glide my mouth along her jawline. While I taste her skin, dragging my tongue upward little by little, I begin to breathe harder—just like Amy. She rakes her fingers through my hair, tugging until she gets what she wants, pressing my mouth harder against the bare skin of her throat.

"Let's see how long you can keep this up, hotshot," she pants.

I chuckle and slide a hand up from her waist to cup one of her tits. It fits in my palm perfectly, as if her breasts were made for me. As I suckle her pebbled nipple, I tug her even closer. The sweet juices of her desire slicken my flesh and urge me to growl like an animal on the prowl.

"Shit." She bucks on me as I slide a hand between her folds. "Need you inside me, please Charlie, please."

"Goddammit," I snarl. "Need a condom."

I can't bear to push her away, so instead, I clench her to me with one arm while I lean over to find my pants. After a bit of shuffling and cursing, I spring up again—holding a rubber—and grin. "Got it in one, baby."

Amy snatches up the packet, catching her bottom lip between her teeth and letting it go so slowly that I might have a heart attack. "I want to do this for you."

Oh, I will definitely have a heart attack. But I don't give a damn. "Go on, then, Coach. Do it."

She rips the packet open with her teeth and then clasps my stiff dick in one hand. While I watch, mesmerized by her actions, she gradually lowers herself inch by inch, making me hiss in a breath and clench my teeth. Her cream is dribbling down my balls by the time I'm fully sheathed inside her, and I'm so fucking close to climax that I can't even think anymore.

Then Amy astonishes me by tightening her core even more, setting off waves of pleasure like nothing I've felt before. Her inner walls are as smooth as silk, and the way she keeps adjusting the angle of her thrusts is driving me crazy. The sucking sound of our bodies colliding echoes around us and turns me on even more. The downpour hitting the dugout roof, the faint creaking of the bench…it has me on the edge of climax already.

I've never done anything like this in my life.

My hard-ass coach rides me like a wild cowgirl, bucking and shouting, refusing to let up for even a second. It pushes us both toward the edge, dangling on a precipice. We are going to explode and keep on exploding.

But no, I won't let either of us go off yet. Not even if it kills me. I grasp her hips, holding her down so she can't ride me. Her annoyed little cry makes me smirk.

"Charlie, I…oh god, I love your dick. Never stop, please, never stop until you come inside me."

"Don't worry. I won't leave you hanging for long…probably."

She gives me a light slap on the cheek. "You're evil, and I love it."

An idea hits me, and I can't resist it. "Wrap your legs around my back and your arms around my neck."

"Why?"

"Shut up and do it, Keller."

Amy rolls her eyes but follows my order. Once she's wrapped around me, I hoist myself off the bench. Then I peel her limbs away from mine and set her on her knees on the bench, facing the wall. The plump cheeks of her sweet ass distract me, though only for a moment.

"Hands on the wall," I command, growling the words. "And spread your thighs."

She obeys.

I slide my cock between those sweet cheeks and thrust deep into her velvety channel, making her gasp. Amy throws her head back, her nails scraping the wall as I drive into her like a jackhammer. The sound of our bodies merging meshes with the slapping of my balls, but it's even louder now, even faster. I reach around her body to shove two fingers between her drenched folds, rubbing mercilessly, desperate to come—but not before she goes off. Her breath hitches in short, delicious moans that make my blood burn even hotter.

"Don't stop, Charlie, never ever stop!" she screams. "Fuck me harder, please, oh shit, please!"

What do I do? I stop, of course. But I still have my dick buried inside her and my fingers covering her clit. I'm torturing myself as much as I am Amy, so it's fair play. I feel as if my whole body might explode into a supernova that will annihilate the universe..

"Please, please, Charlie, please," Amy whines, all her tough-coach bravado suddenly gone. "Let me come, I need it so bad."

Another snarl emerges from me, and then…I hammer into her with so much strength that I swear my eyes roll back in my head. The wooden bench creaks beneath her knees in a rhythm that matches the incoherent sounds that spill from her lips. My groans are building up to a climax with every thrust, mingling with hers as we batter each other in perfect harmony. I slide out almost completely before surging back inside her, the sensation so intense that my vision blurs.

"Harder," she begs, her voice shaking with need, almost whimpering.

Now I'm pounding into her with everything I've got, diving in deeper than ever with a wildly erratic rhythm, high on a kind of elation I've never experienced on the field. Amy's cries rise even higher, and I know she's about to go off at any moment. So am I. Her inner muscles squeeze me torturously as we both barrel toward the finish line. This time, nothing can stop us.

I bury myself inside her with a shout of pure, unadulterated gratification that tumbles from my lips and mingles with hers amid humid night air. Her sex clenches me tightly, and at last, I let go all the way. Electrical currents race down my spine and straight into my cock, pushing me to spill everything inside her lush body. I relinquish myself to the pleasure. Every pulsating blast makes me roar until, finally, I'm spent.

Damn, that was incredible.

Amy leans back against my chest. Her skin is slicked with sweat, her hair drenched—just like mine. For a moment we remain frozen in this position. We're both struggling to catch our breath, and sweat dribbles down our bodies.

Once I've recovered, I sweep her up in my arms. "Time for a shower, Coach."

"Yes, please." She ruffles my damp hair and sniffs my skin. Her nose wrinkles. "You stink, Braddock. We both need that shower, but mostly you."

The slight uptick of her lips assures me she's teasing.

"Pretty sure I heard someone say she was going to see how long I could hold out?"

I feel her smile against my shoulder. "Next time, hotshot."

"You think there's gonna be a next time?"

"Do what your coach says, hotshot." She tugs at a damp lock of my hair. "You drive me wild, Braddock."

"Right back at ya, Keller." I plant a kiss on her temple.

When we get to the bathroom, my fingers shake so much that it takes me forever to twist the handle and get the water running. Amy laughs at my fumbling and tries to help undress me, though she's no steadier. We stumble inside the stall together and revel in the steamy spray.

"You know what this reminds me of?" Her eyes glimmer as brightly as the droplets splashing against her cheeks. "That rain delay last week."

"Except we're both naked," I point out. "And this time you can't claim it's colder than Siberia."

Amy rolls her eyes but steps closer, crowding me into the corner.

What's she up to now? Another mind-blowing fuck, naturally. And my coach won't let me go until I've satisfied her in every conceivable way. But one thought bothers me.

Was this a one-time thing? Or could it be more?

Chapter Eight
Midnight Practice

The training facility is supposed to be empty this time of night. Just me and the stars and my fastball. Shadows should be my only company, but a figure hovering near the dugout proves otherwise. It's Amy, buried in charts, her ponytail a slash of brown amid the dim light. I pause, taking in the unexpected sight.

Ever since our scorching sex in the dugout last week, Amy won't even look me in the eye, much less talk to me. On that night, she ran away—literally—without even saying goodbye. Women confuse the hell out of me. Well, it's not like I wanted a relationship. Did I?

The answer to my own question baffles me. That's not a good sign.

But today, I realize we need to talk about that night. So, I clear my throat. "Couldn't sleep?"

Amy jerks her head up, eyes wide. Her shock wears off swiftly. I don't know whether to feel relieved or uneasy about her reaction. Either way, we need to talk things out.

She tucks a stray hair behind her ear. "Charlie? I thought I'd be the only one crazy enough to come here this late."

I edge closer, trying to read the papers she's huddled over. "What are you doing?"

"Checking your recovery stats," she replies, not missing a beat. Her gaze is cool, her voice measured. "You're behind schedule, you know."

I let out a breath that's part laugh, part relief. "Couldn't sleep either, huh? Thought maybe pitching a few would help me."

Her attention flicks back to the charts. "You've got to take it easy with that shoulder. Otherwise, it won't be just sleep you're losing."

I don't know why, but hearing her concern almost makes me feel better. Almost. I cross my arms, trying to act casual, like being in this kind of limbo doesn't eat me alive. "Nice to know I'm keeping you busy."

Her lips quirk in a faint smile, but there's something behind it, like she wants to say more but doesn't. "I'm always busy, Braddock."

No more "Charlie, please, make me come." Nope, we're back to "Braddock" and chilly glances.

"Honestly, my shoulder is a lot better. Phil agrees. He told me so yesterday."

We stand here, the silence hanging heavily between us. I feel the pull to say something, anything that might break through whatever wall she's put up between us. "You were a kid in the dugout, right?"

The question seems to catch her off guard, but her confusion quickly turns to something gentler. "Grew up there. Just like you, probably."

"Dreamed of being the best," I admit. "Aiming for Cooperstown from the time I could hold a bat, desperate to make it into the Hall of Fame."

"With all the progress you've made with your shoulder, you'll be back on track soon."

I shrug and change the topic. "Living up to your dad's legacy…is that why you do it? Coaching, I mean."

Her gaze is unwavering, though she isn't looking at me. She stares into nothing, with the intensity of a pitcher staring down a batter. "I owe my father that much."

I nod as if I understand the kind of pressure that makes her work herself raw. And maybe I do get it. We aren't so different, after all. Baseball has been my world for as long as I can remember. But right now, I need to push for an answer concerning one vital question.

So, I shove my hands into my pants pockets. "Amy, why did you run away after we, uh, had sex in the dugout."

Amy bows her head, scribbling something on her clipboard. "We had great sex, it's over, there's nothing else to say. We could both get in big trouble for what we did."

"I won't tell anybody."

She flips a page over on her clipboard, studying it briefly, and then looks up at me. "How about we start with something light? No need to throw yourself back on the injured list."

Discussion over, that's what she's saying. "Thanks for worrying about me, Coach."

Amy shrugs one shoulder. "Nothing I wouldn't do for anyone else."

That's not exactly what I want to hear, but now isn't the time for a serious talk. "Lead the way, Coach."

The night is quiet except for our footsteps and the steady buzz of the fluorescent lights. I try a few stretches, and my shoulder is tight but manageable. Amy watches from a short distance away. Her gaze follows my movements as if she's already diagnosing the problem, determining how much better I've gotten—or how much worse. She joins me shortly, demonstrating a few exercises that seem almost ridiculous but actually work.

"Keep your elbow up," she instructs, mimicking a pitching motion.

"Got it." I try to match her precision, testing my arm a bit more even while I hide the wince that comes with it. "What do you think? The old man's still got it, huh?"

She shakes her head. "Don't be so sure about that. If you get overconfident and try to throw a fastball before you're ready, you might injure yourself even worse."

"Thanks for the pep talk, Coach." The sarcasm in my voice is unmistakable, though I hadn't meant to sound that way. Amy's pessimistic attitude threatens to infect me too. But I refuse to let that happen.

To either of us.

"I'm being realistic, Charlie. Not many players make it past thirty before they need to retire."

Did she just call me Charlie? Not Braddock? Hmm, I'm beginning to think she's way more worried about my injury than she's letting on. Why else would she vacillate between calling me Charlie or Braddock? The only explanation I can come up with is a dumb one.

I roll the ball between my hands. "Any advice for a washed-up pitcher, Coach?"

"Take it slow. But don't give up."

"Could say the same for you."

She almost smiles, which I take as a positive sign. "How about a real warm-up? Test those skills a little?"

"Yeah, why not."

We move through the exercises, a series of throws that feel better with every movement. The tension melts away, replaced by a connection that grows with every catch as both of us focus on the game. And on each other too, though not in a romantic way. Amy gives me pointers as needed and lets me do my own thing too. For a moment, it's like everything else fades. Just the ball, the glove, and this fragile thing between us.

Then I hear something.

A whistle. Off-key and deliberately obnoxious.

Groaning, I throw my head back and hiss, "Jared."

He strides up to me like he owns the place, all swagger and cockiness, his voice echoing as he draws closer. "Still awake at this hour, Chucky?"

I don't respond, but I do clench my fist around the ball.

Jared grins, clapping me on the shoulder like we're best pals. Like he's not here strictly to screw with my head. "Insomnia sucks, huh? Must be super worried about our next matchup." He glances at Amy, raising an eyebrow. "What a shame to waste that hot body on coaching a has-been. Or is it babysitting?"

Amy's eyes narrow, and her posture stiffens. "Not now, Morris."

"Didn't realize I was interrupting something." His knowing gaze shifts between Amy and me. "Come on, Coach Keller. Show me how to pitch a fastball after hours."

The innuendo in his tone rankles—not just me, but Amy too. I can tell by the way her lips pucker slightly. As much as I want to tell him off, to throw his words back in his face, Amy gets there first. "We're busy, Jared. Go bother someone else."

He's enjoying this too much to leave quickly, though. His exaggerated sigh makes that clear. "Working with Chucky has made you no fun at all. Guess I'll let you get back to your, uh, workout." He tips his ball cap at me. "See you on the field, Braddock. If you make it that far."

As badly as I want to clock him in the face, I refuse to stoop to Jared's methods.

He finally walks away, whistling all the while.

Amy turns to me. "You okay?"

"Absolutely. That guy's got a gift for getting under my skin, that's all."

She studies me for a moment, then her posture relaxes. "Ready to pick up where we left off?"

I try to find that zone again, the one I'd achieved before Jared barged in, but it takes time. Amy's still here to guide me, fortunately. We return to the field, easily reclaiming our earlier focus. I suspect that's only possible because of the rapport we have, or at least, used to have before the dugout-sex incident.

Amy leaves before I do.

By the time I walk out of the facility, it's coming up on three o'clock—in the morning. The air is chilly, stinging my face as I make my way back to my car. My shoulder aches, but it's a good kind of pain and not as intense as it once had been. The kind that says yeah, I can do this.

And it's because of Amy Keller.

While I climb the stairs to my apartment, the hallway is empty and silent. I push the door open, still reflecting on the night and Amy. Her voice, her eyes, the tolerant smile she gives me whenever I crack an inappropriate joke. The way she seems to understand me like nobody else can.

A sharp knock jerks me out of my thoughts. I hesitate, then pull the door open wider.

My ex-wife stands there, looking like she's just stepped off a magazine cover. It's been a long time since I saw her in person, and the sight stuns me. Why is Alicia here at three in the morning?

"Hello, Charlie," she coos, a half-smile playing on her lips. "Surprised to see me?"

Damn straight I am. But I don't say that. Instead, I step aside to let her in, my mind racing with crazy thoughts about what her unexpected arrival means. I keep my hand on the doorknob, twisting it side to side. "What do you want this time, Alicia? I'm wiped out from midnight practice."

My ex-wife sashays closer. "I want to talk about us. Our future."

"You divorced me, so there is no future for us." I wave toward the open door. "Get out. Now. I'm in no mood for your bullshit. You can walk away on your own, or I can toss you out myself."

She pats my cheek. "I'll call you tomorrow, honey."

Alicia sashays out the door. I slam it after her. If my life gets any screwier, I'll need to get fitted for a straitjacket

Chapter Nine
Rival's Challenge

This morning, Amy gave me the best speech ever—just for me. It was like something out of a movie—rousing, and in a strange way, patriotic. Baseball is America's favorite pastime, after all. I've heard coaches give inspiring speeches before, but Amy's should be written down and enshrined in the Baseball Hall of Fame.

I hear her words replaying in my mind as she leads me out of the locker room.

"Charlie Braddock, you are the Admirals' all-star pitcher for a reason. And when we're on the road to the World Series, I need you in top form. Don't let one idiot's taunts get in your head. Charlie, you are more than ready. This team would be toast without you, the fastball king."

She made me feel like I'm Superman without the cape.

"Maybe you think of baseball as a contest," she continued. "And you're partially right. It's true that in a game one team wins, and another loses. It's true that some players are traded and others get to stay. Some go down to the minors again, and others stick around. Maybe fate plays a role, and luck too."

I had been mesmerized by the fire inside her, the desire to convince me I can be the fastball phenom I was before my injury.

"But sometimes," Amy went on, "things happen that make us question all our assumptions. My dad was the best coach anyone could hope for. Taught me everything I know about being a coach—and he was an encyclopedia of baseball knowledge. Ever since I was six years old, there was nothing I liked more than sitting in the dugout with him, watching him work, listening to what he told his players, enjoying the banter between innings."

Amy was electrifying, and I swore I could almost hear the crowd cheering and whooping.

"But then something happened that changed everything," she goes on. "I think you know what I'm talking about. Dad got sick and passed away too soon. I had a choice: Take over his responsibilities as everyone expected—or step away. Hurtling into the unknown, redefining my own life instead of living up to other people's expectations. It sucked, and it was scary, but I did my best—and now here I am, coaching for a team that kicks ass—and a pitcher who has turned these players into a family."

I couldn't wipe the grin off my face. Her words hit me like a fast-ball to the chest. But she wasn't quite finished yet. "So, what about you, Charlie? You've had some bad luck. Maybe some jerk thinks you're done for the season—or forever. But are you ready to believe that? Or are you going to surprise everyone, including yourself, and come back stronger?"

Amy pretended she wasn't soft on me but—and this was the best part of her speech as well as my favorite bit—she finished by kissing me.

Her voice is still ringing in my ears as she drags me over to the trainer's facility for more heat and ice. That seems unnecessary since my shoulder is already feeling so good that I'm not worried about get-ting hurt again. I'll be careful, of course. But the fear is fading away more every day.

When we exit the facility, three reporters are waiting outside the building. They're clearly hoping to catch a good sound bite they can splash on every TV screen and newspaper headline. Those vultures must be here about yesterday's contest with Jared. I try to brush past the reporters, but they ambush me like gnats in July.

"Charlie! Heard you're back for good!" someone shouts, shoving a mic in my face.

I glance at Amy. She stands with her arms crossed, daring me to stay on script.

"Getting my strength back more every day," I proclaim. "Coach

Keller and the team are making sure I don't overdo it. But I feel good, real good."

Another reporter cuts in. "What about your little showdown yesterday? Looked like Morris was giving you a run for your money."

"I don't pay attention to Jared's trash talk," I lie, feeling Amy's gaze burn into me.

The Aspen Altitude team, our nemeses, often practice in the same facility. So naturally, Morris had to harass me. And yeah, I got a little…irritated. Okay, I shouted obscenities at the jackass because he insulted Amy, and that led to a brief dust-up. I know I need to keep my emotions in check, just like Amy keeps telling me. But it's tough when she's Jared's target.

The third reporter is relentless. "So can Admirals fans expect you at the top of the rotation this season?"

I pause just long enough for Amy to chime in. "Charlie's on a great recovery track. We're making sure he's ready to lead this team all the way to the top."

She's prepared to play bodyguard as the questions keep coming. Amy ushers me toward the parking lot where my car waits like an escape vehicle. I duck around Amy and fire off a parting shot toward the little crowd. "I'll be on the mound soon, better than ever!"

The reporters scribble furiously, shout, and circle like buzzards over fresh roadkill. I can still hear them when we reach my car.

"Did you see the camera guy wearing the Altitude's jersey?" Amy asks. "That's either dedication—or a pay-off."

"It wouldn't surprise me if Morris has him on his payroll," I agree, sliding into the driver's seat.

Amy jumps in and sits beside me, seeming like she's choosing her next words carefully. "Do you think you're ready for Aspen this weekend?"

"I just told them—"

"You told them what they wanted to hear." She moves into her patented resolute stance, daring anyone who has the balls to challenge her to give it a go. "Can you handle Morris in a real game or not?"

"I'll be fine. Don't you trust me anymore?"

"Yes, but your injury sapped your confidence for a while." She drills her gaze directly into mine. "You've done amazingly well when you practice with your teammates, but winning against a rival team is much more stressful."

"Amy, I meant what I said. My shoulder can handle it." I glance at her sideways as I maneuver the car out of the lot. "Don't you believe I can do it?"

"I believe you're still a stubborn idiot."

She sounds annoyed, but I catch the hint of a smile before she turns away to stare out the window. "Just don't blow it, okay? A lot's riding on you and your first spring training matchup."

I groan. "Let it go, Amy."

"You know I can't do that."

She acts like she doesn't believe I can get the job done, that I might crack under pressure though I never have before. Something else is going on inside her head. And suddenly, a proverbial light bulb pops on over my head. Maybe my epiphany is bullshit, but I don't think so.

We're on the road now, and she's already running through scenarios for this weekend's game. I'm visualizing finally burning Jared with a smoking fastball as he stands there slack-jawed. I don't say much, just nodding along, partly listening. Mostly, I'm imagining her saying something else when we get back to my place. Something like "you really kicked his ass out there."

Instead, she's still talking about expectations.

Halfway to my apartment building, I can't contain my epiphany any longer. I peek at her sideways. "You're still worried about me, aren't you? That's why you've been such a downer about my healing progress."

"Don't be ridiculous."

Her stubborn expression tells me she won't admit to the truth, not yet. The rest of the drive passes in silence as she contemplates the view out the window again, and I obsess over what the Altitudes' lineup might look this year. I heard a couple of guys defected to other teams, but I don't know if that's true.

We've just reached my apartment building, and I've pulled into a curbside parking slot. Amy jumps out before I can even stop completely.

"I'll email you the schedule, Braddock," she says over her shoulder.

I lean across the seat. "Amy, wait, we need to—"

She waves her hand in the air without looking back and disappears into her car, where she'd left it along the curb. Her taillights are receding into the distance before I can even climb out of my vehicle.

Back inside my apartment, I head straight for the freezer and fish out a couple of Miller Lites, then crash on the couch and flip on the TV. Naturally, the news is all about yesterday's dust-up with Jared and my impending "comeback." The talking heads are already at it, rambling on about how I'll be lucky if I can keep up with the camera crew, let alone Morris.

I crack a beer open and choose to ignore all their BS predictions.

The news cuts to a clip of Amy during the final game against the Marlins, which had been last year. She wasn't my coach back then. In the clip, I can see her ponytail pulled tight and bouncing around. Then the video switches to her on the field yesterday, stepping between me and my nemesis like she's managing two wild dogs instead of players fighting for dominance.

I couldn't say it in front of all those reporters, but I know how much she's banking on me pulling off this comeback. That only makes me want it more—maybe more than anything in my life.

Forget about Morris. Focus on your game, Braddock. The jerk wants you off guard.

Tomorrow, I'm slated to face off against Jared again, for the first time in more than a year. Am I nervous? Nah, of course not. Well, maybe a tiny bit. But I have the best incentive of all to keep me grounded and focused.

Her name is Amy Keller.

The next morning, I wake up before the alarm and do a quick stretching routine to gauge how my shoulder feels. Nothing hurts— a good sign. Grabbing a protein bar and a banana, I head out the door, determined to get in some solo training before my early meeting with Amy. By the time she arrives, clipboard in hand, I've already run through half of my usual warm-ups.

She sweeps her gaze over me from head to toe. "Someone's eager today."

"Just getting ready to smash the Assitudes."

I expect her to roll her eyes at the nickname, but she only sighs. "Cut the wisecracks, Braddock. Today, you need to prove to the world that you're still the fastball king. Let's get started."

Chapter Ten

The Scouting Report

The cramped office is cluttered with stats and scores as well as a few moldy old baseballs that are long past their expiration date. When I'd first been injured, I'd felt like a relic of bygone days, of victories I might never achieve again. But I've realized lately that this isn't my final inning. Amy, on the other hand, remains anxious about my first game since my injury—and that anxiety rolls off her in unseen waves. I can feel those waves, though, and they're infecting me too.

I never would've guessed my tough coach would be biting her nails over me.

For the rest of the day, I steer clear of Phil's office, not ready to face him just yet. I've never been able to read the manager's mind or even his expression, but he's never been malicious. I shouldn't worry. Besides, he wouldn't fire me before my first post-injury game. So I hit the gym, throwing my energy into a brutal workout, pushing until my muscles scream like they're ready to mutiny.

Eventually, exhaustion wins out. I trudge back to the locker room to find it empty except for the hum of a vending machine and the smell of sweat that lingers in the air.

A crumpled scouting report lies on the desk, mocking me with stats and figures that suggest one of two things. Phil is measuring my mediocrity, or he's telling the team owner to ditch me right away. Ray is a nice guy, but this is business to him. Yeah, I've heard rumors that they want to trade me, and it's no joke. Amy was involved in those discussions, but I have no clue what she told the big guys—or what they told her.

I pick up the crumpled sheet and smooth it out. The words on the page make my jaw clench. Send Braddock back to the minors now, he's toxic.

Who wrote those words? No idea. It couldn't be Amy.

I crush the paper in my fist and hurl it across the room. As I storm into the hallway, a familiar voice shouts, "Stop, Charlie!"

I freeze, turning to face Amy.

She stands in the corridor like she knows I'm already a goner. My coach has the look of someone about to execute me in the most merciful way. She must think Jared will whup my ass, and I'll lead the Admirals to a devastating defeat. I remember the last time our team played against the Altitude, and how Jared grinned at me from third base like he was already three plays ahead, already knowing exactly how the game would end.

"See you next season, Braddock. Or maybe not!" he'd called out while grinning and blowing a kiss at me like a true shithead.

I glare at Amy. "Did you know about this report?"

She doesn't flinch or even shrug. Her arms are barred over her chest like armor, but the concern in her eyes looks real. "Yes, I found out this morning."

"They're sending me back to the minors."

"No, not yet. You have one chance to prove you're still the star pitcher."

"Were you part of this plan to send me down to the minors?" I clench the paper tighter, making it crinkle in my palm. A breath gusts out of my nostrils, and I pitch the crumpled sheet across the room.

Amy's eyes widen, not with guilt but something else. Something that cuts into me like a hot knife. She steps closer.

"Forget about the scouting report." Amy nods toward the paper I destroyed. "Look at these improvements. Your ERA has dropped. Your fastball velocity is up by eight percent." Her tone is assertive, sure, like she's talking down a rookie on the edge of a meltdown. "I believe in you, not numbers."

I want to believe her, for sure. I need to believe. But the report feels like a death sentence, and she's holding the gavel. "If that's true, why was the report hidden in Phil's office?"

She pauses, and it's a loaded silence that lets me know she's digging deep to keep her cool. "Maybe because someone didn't want you to see it. Maybe because they wanted you focused on what you can do rather than what a sheet of paper tells you."

What she said makes sense. It's all she's been saying since the injury. It's all she's been wanting from me since the day she waltzed into my life. I need her to believe in me. Isn't that pathetic?

"Focus isn't the problem," I explain. "It's the fact that I'm getting iced. I can feel it. But I'm the last one to know, like always."

Her expression doesn't change, but there's a flicker of something in her eyes that I can't decipher. She steps closer, past the line of distance she usually keeps between us, the one that's been there since the night we had sex in the dugout.

"The only one who doesn't believe in you, Charlie, is you."

I let out a bitter laugh. "Maybe I've got a reason not to."

Amy's lips flatten, a sure sign she's frustrated. "Ray threw that paper away because he still believes in you, and he's giving you a chance to prove that faith is warranted. Phil believes in you too, and so do I. The only one who's lost faith is you."

The accusation hangs in the air like a foul ball, its spin undecided. "You can't pretend you haven't thought about life without me dragging the team down."

"I don't need to pretend anything." Her voice has an edge now, the kind that slices clean. "You know what I've thought about, Charlie? You running down bases. You back at the top of your game. You carrying your team to a World Series victory."

I'm pacing, my feet slapping on the linoleum, every step matching the frantic beat of my heart. I can't stop moving, like if I do, everything will catch up to me and crash over me in a tsunami of regrets.

"Look at the numbers again," she pleads. "This isn't about getting rid of you. It's about you turning it around the way you've always done before—until you met me."

I halt mid-step, rotating my head to stare at her. My heart pounds as if this moment could change everything, for better or worse. "What are you saying, Amy?"

She rubs her arms, avoiding my gaze. "You don't need me anymore. Your fastball is back, and you'll lead your team to glory, I know you will."

Amy thinks I don't need her? She's crazy. I never would've been on the verge of a comeback without her. I reach her in two strides, grasping her shoulders, pulling her so close that our breaths mingle. "What happened in that meeting? Tell me, Amy, please."

She worries her lip as tears begin to gather in her eyes. But she straightens and lifts her chin, wiping away the wetness. Amy meets my gaze head-on. "Don't you get it? That sheet of paper was crumpled because Phil convinced Ray not to trade you or send you back to the minors. As for me…"

"What about you?"

"Ray ordered Phil to fire me."

"What?" The solitary syllable came out as a half-whisper. "But you're my coach. They can't fire you right before our first big game."

Amy shakes her head. "Ray is one tough bastard. When he makes a decision, it's final."

I don't know what to say. Too many words crowd my mind. Too much is coming at me all at once. Ray ordered Phil to fire Amy? He's nuts. She's the best damn coach the Admirals have ever had. I study her freshly wiped eyes, the sudden calm in her features, and that's when it fully sinks in. She's made her peace with the situation.

"Why didn't you tell me, Amy?"

She pulls a tissue out of her pocket and gently blows into it. Then she squares her shoulders. "This is your one chance to show Ray you still belong in the major leagues. My dismissal shouldn't stand in the way of your success."

The implication makes me wince. Amy thinks I'm better off without her, that's clear. But I could never have come this far on my own after my injury.

"No way," I insist. "You're coming with me to every game—as my coach. Otherwise, I quit."

She draws in a slow, ragged breath and hesitates just long enough for doubt to creep back in. Then she rips it away with words that sound like they sear her throat. "I can't let you do that, Charlie."

I gape at her, the shock twisting into anger. "You can't stop me."

Despite her bleary eyes, her voice remains firm. "This team is your life. I'm just a coach you had a fling with."

She's trying to make it sound like it never mattered, like she never cared, but I know better. "I thought you were the one who told me not to give up."

Amy swallows hard, and for a second, I think she might change her mind. But then she looks at me like she's engraving my face in her memory. The finality in her gaze hits me harder than any pitch ever could.

"I'll be fine," she assures me, her voice barely above a whisper.

I stagger backward a step, my mind racing to find something, anything, to say. Words tangle in my throat, refusing to come out.

"Amy," I manage at last, her name loaded with everything I want to say and can't.

She says nothing, simply watching me. The silence stretches between us until it snaps something inside me.

"Fine," I spit out, sounding bitter and broken even to my own ears.

With a last look, one filled with too much feeling for me to bear, she walks away. Everything inside me wants to run after her, make her listen until she understands. But I can't move, can't think. The world's spinning like a wild pitch careening toward the dirt.

Phil's office door slams shut behind her.

"Charlie! There you are!" Jared's voice snaps me out of my trance. He strides down the hall like he owns the place.

"What do you want, Morris?"

"To grab a beer with my favorite rival." Jared leans against the wall, smirking.

I'm not in the mood for his crap. "Get lost."

Jared saunters away, whistling the song "Take Me Out to the Ballgame."

That jerk means nothing to me. I need Amy back—now—and I know exactly how to make that happen.

Chapter Eleven
Return to the Mound

This might be the biggest night of my life. Sure, I've pitched my fair share of awesome fastballs but tonight feels different, special—for reasons both good and bad. If I can't convince Phil and Ray to keep Amy as my coach for good…I don't know what I'll do. She could be my groupie, I guess. But that's not too appealing either.

She wouldn't go for that, anyway.

But for this one day, this one last time, Amy will serve as my coach. If I can win this game for my team and make it a blowout, maybe she will change her mind about leaving.

I tug my cap on and scan the crowd gathered here tonight. I love a good night game. The cool air, the bright lights, the crowd, it's everything I love about the game. As I breathe in the smells, from grass to hot dogs, all of it bolsters me like nothing else can. This is my world. Once both teams are on the field and the fans settle into their seats, I feel the rush of adrenaline kicking in—almost enough to tune out the tension between my shoulder blades.

The Aspen Altitude are in town. Not all of those guys are dicks, but quite a few are. Jared Morris has his own clique within the Altitude roster. These games always get heated, which is exactly what I need tonight to rev me up. I take the mound and toss a warm-up pitch. The ball smacks into the catcher's mitt with a satisfying thud. Good start. Phil and Ray are watching from the sidelines, whispering to each other like they're picking out a puppy—or they're deciding which minor league team they want to dump me in.

"Focus, Charlie," Amy calls out from her spot near the dugout.

"Hey, shouldn't you be home knitting a sweater?" I yell back with a smirk.

Her lips tighten into a line, but I catch a flicker of humor in her eyes before she turns away. That's right, Amy, watch what I can do. If I've still got my mojo, then Amy will pounce on me the second the game is over. Hot sex for Charlie tonight? Damn, I hope so.

But Amy swore she'd quit being my coach after this game. I'll prove to her she can't quit. Somehow, some way, no matter what Phil and Ray might've said.

The batter steps up to the plate, and I struggle to maintain a neutral expression when I actually want to grin at Amy and make rude faces at the Assitudes. Yeah, that's a little childish. But I'm feeling the groove for the first time in months, and the vibe is amazing. It takes a second for me to realize who's facing off with me.

It's Jared Morris, batting in the number one spot tonight.

Someone's gotten cocky. His smirk tells me without words that he thinks I've lost it. But before he can open his smart mouth, I wind up and hurl the ball with everything I've got.

The satisfying sound of a strike zipping past him fills the night air. Jared's grin fades just a bit as he turns to Amy in mock surprise.

"Looks like you taught him more than knitting," the jackass quips loud enough for everyone to hear.

Oh, it's on now. I throw another fastball, watching Jared flinch ever so slightly before he swings and misses.

The crowd eats it up, roaring with every pitch. My shoulder protests with a dull ache, but I tune it out. You're in good shape, Charlie, but don't get overconfident.

My next pitch is the one Jared's been waiting for, and he smacks it toward left field. I hold my breath as our fielder bolts for the ball, snagging it just before it hits the ground. Jared jogs back to the dugout, shaking his head like it's all a big joke. Meanwhile, Amy's watching me with an expression I can't read. Satisfaction? Concern? I'm going with satisfaction.

The next few batters are a blur of strikes and easy outs. Every successful pitch boosts my confidence. We're up by three runs by the end of the second inning, and my self-assurance is soaring. If we keep up this pace, Amy won't stand a chance at saying no to staying with me.

Then, maybe ten minutes into the third, I feel it—an insistent throb moving through my shoulder and right down to my fingertips. The ache I was ignoring. It's back with a vengeance.

Fuck.

Amy catches my eye from her spot on the bench and taps her head, the signal to use my brain.

Slow down, pace yourself, don't be an idiot. I give Amy a curt nod and then hurl another pitch with everything I've got. The bat connects, a line drive past second base. Jared's on first, looking back at me with that stupid, knowing grin. My shoulder screams for me to stop, but I don't care. The stadium lights seem brighter suddenly, making it hard for me to focus on the catcher's signals. My vision blurs slightly, and for the first time tonight, anxiety creeps in.

Don't doubt yourself now, just power through it. But every pitch loses some heat. The next batter walks. Then another hits. Double play keeps us alive for a few outs before we're finally back in the dugout. I can't even look at Amy as she calls me over to her.

"You need to slow down, Charlie," she urges, grasping my arm. Her voice is firm but laced with worry. "It's not worth getting injured again."

My throat tightens as I pull away from her grip. Am I ignoring the truth I don't want to admit? That I'm afraid I'll never get back to what I used to be?

"I'm fine," I insist, almost growling the words. My vanity won't let me say more.

She gives me a long, searching look that feels more like a lecture than any words could convey. "Phil can call in someone else."

"Not happening." I grab a water bottle and guzzle down the whole contents, keeping my eyes anywhere except on her.

But inside, I'm panicking.

Me, the fastball king.

This was supposed to be my comeback, the night when everything falls back into place. Instead, every inning drags me deeper into self-doubt. The fourth inning starts off rocky. My velocity's way down, and the Assitudes take full advantage. Three runs in quick succession before we finally put a stop to their rally.

My shoulder feels like I have hot coals imbedded in there, and my mind's flooded with worst-case scenarios. Cut from the roster. Shipped off to God knows where. Amy leaving, just like she said she would if I can't make my pitches count. I slump onto the bench after the disastrous inning, avoiding eye contact with everyone. I can feel their judgment burning into me and I can taste my own failure in the air.

Jared makes the rounds in their dugout.

"Not bad for a dude with one arm!" he shouts across the field, riling up his teammates further.

The asshole's not wrong.

"Charlie," Amy calls out, but I shake my head before she can remind me to be smart and strategic.

"I need one more inning," I announce, cutting her off, barely recognizing my own strained voice.

"No—"

"One more inning!" Shouting isn't enough to convince her, but desperation might be. "I can come back from this. You know I can."

She watches me carefully, trying to gauge if it's bullshit bravado or if there's anything left in my tank worth fighting for.

"Okay, one more." Her tone makes it clear it's a reluctant concession. "But Charlie, I swear—"

I'm already halfway back to the mound.

I focus on stretching my arm, anything to dull the pain. If this inning craters too, I'm done for, and Amy's out the door. The first batter digs in, confident in a way that shoots anger straight through me. He fouls off two pitches before popping an easy fly ball into our center fielder's glove.

One down.

By the fourth batter, I'm running on fumes. I fire another pitch, ignoring the shooting pain when Jared smashes a double into left field. He stands there with that same conceited grin while I grind through three more hitters. Finally, we're out of the inning, but just barely. The score's tied, and I've got nothing left. As soon as Phil pulls me off the mound for good, I stumble toward the locker room, drowning out the crowd's chant of the new pitcher's name. No one says anything as I limp down the tunnel, but I can practically hear their thoughts.

Washed up. Done for. Lost the fire.

Once I'm inside the locker room, I slump against a locker and let out a shaky breath. My shoulder feels like it's been smashed to pieces. Maybe it has. Amy's words echo in my head—you need to slow down, it's not worth getting injured again—but I've ignored her so many times she probably thinks I'm a lost cause. I throw my glove across the room and watch it bounce off a wall with a hollow thud.

My heart sinks when Amy walks in. The drawn look on her face tells me how this conversation will go down.

"Charlie," she says softly, but there's firmness in her voice too. "We need to talk."

My shoulders slump even more. Because I'm screwed.

Chapter Twelve
The Setback

Amy's expression is full of fury as she slams the locker room door shut behind us. For a moment, she just glares at me with her hands on her hips and her eyes narrowed, tapping her fingers. "What the hell were you doing out there? You weren't the only player on the field, Braddock. If you can't play smarter than that, you won't play at all."

I can't help feeling defensive, but lashing out at her seems unwise, to say the least. I'm still sweaty from the game, but I don't dare grab a towel, not when Amy is on a rampage. She won't let up until she's said her piece. So, I lean against a row of lockers, trying to appear more relaxed than I feel.

"I was trying to win," I say. "Kinda thought that was the point of the game."

Amy's glare could cut glass. "Not at the expense of your shoulder, Braddock. We need you in for the season, not just one damn game."

I almost laugh. She's worried about my shoulder? If only she knew the truth. It isn't only my arm that's messed up. It's my confidence too. Amy's leaving me behind to go somewhere else. "You need me? Since when?"

"Since it's my job to care. I'm your coach, dammit."

"Then coach me." I throw my hands up in mock surrender. "But you might want to decide if you like my arm in working order or hanging limp. Kind of hard to have both."

She blusters a breath out through her nostrils, but there's a flicker of something else now, something deeper, in that expression. "This is not a joke, Charlie. You push yourself like that again, and you'll be out for good."

She's standing so close that I can almost feel the heat radiating off her body. The thought of being out of the game makes my stomach twist, but I can't show her that. Not yet.

"Don't need to ride me so hard," I tell Amy, brushing past her to yank my jersey over my head. "If I go soft, I lose my edge. Either you believe I know what I'm doing, or you don't. Make up your mind."

She shakes her head, disbelief written all over her face. "Have you thought this through at all? Because right now, it looks like you're squandering your career."

"Come on, it's not that big a deal." I try for a joking tone as I add, "If you knock me out of one game, I'll get a mini vacation. St. Barts has always sounded nice."

"This is serious!" Her voice rises, echoing off the walls.

I notice the way her ponytail sways as she paces. Even when she's furious, she moves with purpose, like everything she does has a reason. Like it's her goddamn mission to make sure I don't screw up my life.

Slumping my shoulders, I rub my forehead. "Fine. I'll take it down a notch if that makes you happy." I slam my locker shut and face her. "But don't bench me just because you're afraid I might break a nail."

The way she stares me down, it's like she's peeling back my defenses layer by layer. It's unnerving. "You think this is about me? I'm trying to make sure you have a career after this season." She tempers her voice, just a touch. "You used to be the best, Charlie. I want to help you get back there. But you've got to stop pushing so hard, otherwise you might damage your shoulder irreparably."

Her determination and dire tone throw me off balance. Those words hang between us like a curveball I didn't see coming.

When I study her, deeply and rationally, I realize she means every word. "That's why you're still here, right? For me? Except you're leaving after this game."

Amy crosses her arms, the fire still in her eyes. "You'll have nothing left if you keep going like this. Just think about it, okay? About what's really important."

I don't know whether she's talking about my shoulder or something else, but she's got me wondering all the same. I watch as she heads for the door, her strides as determined as ever. Once she's gone, the locker room is quiet except for the dull thud of my heart. This isn't only about the game anymore.

Maybe it never was.

As I exit the stadium, I hear the color commentator informing the crowd that I'm out for this game—and explaining why.

The fans can guess the rest. Amy's heading back to her apartment in Jacksonville and then probably on to…wherever she used to live. Christ, I never even thought to ask about that. I'm not exactly keen on watching Jared act like God's gift to baseball, so I run a hand through my hair and speed past the parking lot.

About a mile down the main road, I hit a sports bar called The Fly Ball Pub. The place feels just as shaken as I am after that last play—half the neon letters on the pub's sign are burned out. The remaining letters flicker with a headache-inducing red light. Inside, there's some talk about me mixed with clinking glasses and rowdy cheers for the Altitude. I suck it up and slide onto an empty stool. Jared might have won this round, but if Amy thinks I'm sitting out, she doesn't know me as well as she thinks.

"Scotch," I tell the bartender, a lanky guy who looks barely old enough to serve drinks. His name tag says he's Dave.

"Rough game out there, huh?" Dave smirks as he slides the glass over to me.

"You could say that." I take a long sip, letting the burn distract me from the mess inside my head.

"Guess you're getting an early start on your vacation," he adds with a grin.

"If you can call a couple days off a vacation."

I bet Jared put everyone up to this before even leaving the field, making sure the word would spread like wildfire—Braddock's out. Dave is probably friends with Morris. I struggle not to grit my teeth, feeling like I've got a bullseye on my back.

"Bet you could do with a break from the crowds," Dave says, leaning back and taking in the game as a roar goes up from the pub crawlers in here. "Sounds good to me. Downtime in St. Barts would be sweet."

The Altitude scores again, and just like that, the place erupts. Baseball jerseys and foam fingers wave around, though I can't see who's holding them. I down my drink and signal for another. This is how it's gonna be until I prove them wrong: Jared soaking up the spotlight and Amy glowering at me.

Stop whining, Braddock. Suck it up and keep going.

I slap a few bills on the bar and ditch this joint.

That night, the pain wakes me up. In the morning, I roll out of bed, barely managing to dress myself before heading for an MRI that promises answers I don't want to hear. Only Phil could get a scan done that quickly. The results aren't what I hoped. Inflammation, weeks of recovery, maybe longer.

Phil paces like an angry bear in the manager's office, threatening to bench me for the season if I don't pull my head out of my ass. My arm's throbbing, and so is my pride. Amy is nowhere to be seen, but I knew she'd be gone by now. Her one-game reprieve has run out.

This morning's practice doesn't feel right—at least to me. I got used to Amy being here, giving me hell, propping me up, whatever it took to prepare me. My new coach, Andy, definitely knows his stuff, but...

I miss Amy. How pathetic is that?

After another long day of rehab and some gentle practice, I go home for the night. As I drop the bottle of painkillers on my nightstand, I flop onto the bed like a rag doll. My shoulder feels stiff even after the meds kick in. They say it'll take weeks to heal, but I don't have that kind of time if I want to stay in the game. If I want to stay relevant.

On day three without Amy, I receive an unwanted visitor. It's Alicia, and she seems determined to play nursemaid, problem-solver, and meddler of the year, all rolled into one.

"Charlie!" she cries out, bursting through the door with a bandwagon's worth of Admirals merch. "I brought you a care package!"

"I'm good, really, so you can leave now." I wish I'd remembered to take away her key to my apartment after the divorce. But I didn't. So, all I can do now is drag myself into a sitting position on the sofa, blinking sleep out of my eyes. She's already stranded me in a sea of swag, and I screw up my face when I see a particular item. "An Admirals onesie? If you're trying to seduce me, that's a terrible way to start."

"Don't be so mopey," she says, her voice sing-songy and bright. "You need to keep yourself busy while you're sidelined."

I wince at the word. "Who says I'm sidelined?"

Her smile wavers, and her brows wrinkle. "Everyone? But that's not necessarily bad news. You're rehabbing, right? Taking it easy like you're supposed to."

"Alicia." I give her my best long-suffering look. "I don't want company right now."

"You aren't planning to do something stupid, are you?"

"What's it matter if I am?"

She lays a hand on my forehead like she thinks I'm feverish. Then my ex-wife settles her ass on the sofa's arm right beside me. "Forget about that Amy girl. I can take care of you better than anyone else."

I slump into the cushions. "Just leave me alone, Alicia, okay?"

She jumps up, hands on her hips. "No, it's not okay. I won't leave your side until you've recovered, and that's nonnegotiable."

I groan. The woman I want has left me, and the ex-wife I don't want refuses to go away. Perfect.

Chapter Thirteen
Rock Bottom

Years have gone by since Alicia Jones decided I wasn't worth her time anymore. Now, I can't seem to get rid of her. Everywhere I turn, there she is offering me a bowl of soup or a box of crackers or, heaven help me, a plush pink blanket to keep me warm. She even tucks me in at night, I swear to God she does. This mothering instinct is starting to get creepy.

Hard to believe I used to sleep with this kooky woman.

I finally put my foot down when she tries to get in the shower with me to help soap me up—in the nude, of course. That's where I draw the line. I slam the shower door shut before she can climb in. "Alicia, you lunatic! Jeez, can't a guy get some privacy?"

She sighs. "You're so finicky, Charlie."

Thankfully, my ex-wife leaves me alone—once I'm fully dressed and ready for today's practice. She did not try to dress me this morning. But she did feed me apple sauce, claiming it's good for my pitching arm. How, exactly? Alicia never explained.

Yeah, this is what they call rock bottom. At least my ex-wife hasn't followed me into the bathroom so she can try to wipe my ass for me.

"I'll wait in the car," she states, pulling up in front of the training facility. The chilly autumn air whips through her blonde hair. She's not staying out in it long enough to mess with that expensive hairdo of hers, though. She shuts the door before I get a chance to respond.

The muscles in my shoulder cramp up a touch as I carefully maneuver myself out of the car. The stupid thing still gives me trouble. It's getting better, but every minute longer it takes to heal seems like an hourglass dripping my career away.

A familiar figure flounces onto the field. Alicia receives wolf whistles from my teammates and clearly enjoys it. So much for her staying in the car. She installs herself near the dugout to watch the team. Alicia has been making sure I get to and from practice as if I can't manage the pain myself. She wasn't this attentive when we were married.

Hell, she wasn't around at all. Her career came first.

I try to shake off the memories of those lonely nights, focusing on the real problem. Why is she suddenly glued to my side? I can't tell if she feels guilty, wants something, or just craves an audience. The truth is, I don't have the heart to send her packing.

Phil greets me inside the locker room, clipboard in hand, just the way Amy had always done.

My throat thickens at the memory of Amy, but I chase it away as best I can.

"How's the shoulder, Charlie?" Phil asks. I can hear the question beneath the question. How much longer before you're back on the field? I give him a noncommittal shrug and try to sound convincing. "It's getting there."

Alicia waltzes in behind me, a gust of chilly air following her. I don't know how to tell her I'm in the middle of a meeting, so I don't bother.

"What time should I come back to pick you up?" she asks, her eyes darting from Phil to me.

"Give me an hour," I say, feeling Phil's eyes burn a hole through my pride.

"Charlie," he starts, "we need you back at one hundred percent." There's an edge to his voice, like he's trying to assuage the burn of a hard truth. "Ray's worried about his investment in you. But he's got faith in your talent. We all do."

Alicia raises a perfectly arched brow. "Does that mean he'll be back in time for opening day or not?"

I rub the back of my neck, feeling the weight of their expectations. "I'm working on it."

Phil gives me a look that suggests he's getting tired of my excuses, and I don't blame him. "We need you fully committed, Charlie. That means no ex-wives clinging on."

My ex-wife bristles. "Of all the nerve—"

"He's right, Alicia. You're, uh, kind of…getting in the way these days. I appreciate that you want to help, but I'm a big boy now. It's inappropriate for you to keep hanging around." I give her hand a light squeeze. "Please go. You've got your own life to live."

She wipes away a few tears, then nods. "Okay, I'm leaving. If you ever need anything—"

"Goodbye, Alicia."

She pivots on her heel with the same cool grace she had when she walked away from our marriage.

As soon as she's out of earshot, Phil aims his best managerial stare at me. "You need to get back to your old self. We need you, but only if your shoulder is ready for away games. The season is about to start, you know."

I get what he's saying. I'm not out of time yet, but the clock is ticking, winding down to Judgment Day.

Phil leans forward, resting his elbows on his thighs, and turns his hardest stare on me. "Your substitute coach wasn't working for you, that much is clear. We need our fastball king in prime condition."

"I know. And my shoulder—"

Phil interrupts with one raised hand. "I've seen your latest scans, which means I probably know your condition better than you do. But here's the deal. You can't get back on the field until you believe you can do it. My opinion is bullshit."

I swallow against a lump in my throat, having no idea what I'm supposed to say.

"Listen up," Phil says. "Because I'll only say this once. You're the best pitcher I've seen, and you can win the World Series this year. That's why I'm giving you a gift."

He stands up, shoves two fingers into his mouth, and lets out the loudest whistle I've ever heard. "Get your ass in here now, Coach!"

The locker-room door swings open—and Amy walks in.

Before my shock has even really set in, Phil pats my shoulder and says, "Here's your gift, Braddock. Don't fuck it up. You have no idea how many favors I had to cash in for this."

I still can't speak even as Phil walks away.

Amy traipses up to me, wearing an expression that's impossible to decipher. "Are you ready to practice like your life depends on it? No whining, no excuses, just grueling practice."

Clearing my throat, I stand up straighter. "I'm ready, Coach."

"You'd better be. Otherwise, I'll have to cancel our weekend trip."

"Where are we going? Zimbabwe?"

She rolls her eyes and straps her arms over those luscious tits. "You won't find out until you've proven to me that you're ready to sweat blood and train until you drop."

"Are you serious?"

"Do I look like I'm pranking you? You're off the bench, but not for long if your form stays like this."

She waves toward the slouch I've somehow fallen into lately.

I fake-wince, trying to mask the thrill I feel with mock resignation. "So, we'll be, what? Stuck together twenty-four seven?"

A ghost of a smile tugs at her lips. "If you can't handle it, now's the time to back out. I hear the sanitation department needs another garbage man."

"And lose my chance to make the opening roster? No way."

She tilts her head. "Charlie, this won't be a vacation or a romantic getaway."

"You can stop whacking my head with a shovel, Amy. I'm not that stupid."

"Good," she says sharply, but with warmth just beneath the surface.

I'd almost forgotten this push and pull is exactly what I thrive on with Amy Keller. Alicia never made me feel this invigorated.

Bracing myself for whatever insane schedule Amy's cooked up, I follow her down the hall to the gym. As she leads the way, I can't resist admiring her ass and the way her tight pants accentuate every delicious curve. I need her for more than training. She's become the most important person in my life, period, and it has very little to do with baseball.

I can't let her down again. I won't. After a fruitful workout, I'm ready to go.

"Okay, what's in store today?" I ask as we step out onto the diamond.

She swivels toward me, already tossing a baseball in my direction. "Show me how you throw these days."

I catch the ball with my good hand and roll my shoulder back as if it doesn't ache like hell. There's no sympathy in her stare, only high expectations. Yeah, I've missed that too.

I wind up and pitch, feeling the muscles scream under the strain, but it feels far less painful today. The ball blasts past Amy before she's even ready for it. The ball makes a loud smack against the backstop and bounces back toward us.

She raises a brow, clearly impressed. "Not bad for an old man."

"Hah-hah. Better not annoy me, Keller." I stride up to her and cup her ass with one hand. "I'm not too old to spank you, kid."

"Are you sure you aren't too elderly to do that?"

"Next you'll be saying I'm washed up."

"If the shoe fits," she says with a teasing glint in her eyes.

"How about I show you another one, Coach?"

"Sounds good," Amy replies, catching the ball on one hop and throwing it back with a fluid motion that reminds me why she's so damn good at this.

I grind through another pitch, a hard fastball with some menace to it. This time she's ready, sidestepping out of the ball's path as it crashes into the backstop.

"Not bad." She winks at me. "Maybe you've still got it after all. Maybe you deserve a mini vacation this weekend."

"Where are we going?"

Her smile could light up the universe. "My hometown, the place where baseball truly lives and breathes—Cooperstown."

"Are you kidding? I've never been there, but I always wanted to go." I sound like a ten-year-old, and I might just start jumping up and down. But I don't care.

Amy laughs, and it's the sweetest sound on earth. "Better start packing right after practice."

She's given me just enough encouragement to give me hope. That small sliver of belief is like sunlight warming me after weeks of clouds. Even though every nerve in my body burns, I brace for another throw.

Maybe I could do this with any one of a thousand other coaches, but none of them would make me feel like I'm ten feet high. Why is that? The answer smacks me like a curveball to my head.

I'm in love with Amy Keller.

Chapter Fourteen
The Trade Rumor

The day before Amy and I will be heading for Cooperstown, I see my worst fear splashed across newspaper headlines and sports radio stations across the country. Well, my second worst fear. My name is on the trade block, and I won't be surprised if that's my fate. It's better than going down to the minors. I'll probably wind up joining the White Sox. Last year, they had their worst season in the history of the team, so I'll fit right in.

Every reporter in the press area is either losing their mind or running in circles. Maybe both. I'm half an hour from showtime, headed into the stadium for our matchup against the Altitude.

Every camera is trained on me and not the field.

"They're talking Philadelphia," one reporter hollers. "They want him bad."

Sure, I believe that. The pitcher with a bum shoulder is wanted by every team. Though I've got my game face on, I think about a dozen reporters see through it already and know I'm toast. Before I can shove through the horde, I hear the familiar voice of Seb Hudson, the only sports anchor who doesn't hate me for being injured.

"The Philadelphia Panthers are ready to trade for Charlie Braddock," Seb announces.

He's usually right about these things. But I pray he's wrong this time. I don't need a fucking sports anchor to tell me the trade makes sense for everyone involved. Every time I step up to the mound lately, I'm batting about .050 under my own weight. That is not good, to put it mildly.

I glance up at the breaking news feeds playing out on TVs near the concessions area. The banner under the anchor says, "The End for Braddock?" and another news ticker declares, "Breaking: Braddock on Trade Block." They're only saying out loud what I've been thinking for months. What I wish was all in my head.

When I finally get into the locker room, I feel like I've survived a pack of sharks that want to devour me alive. My teammates offer encouragement and slaps on the back, but it all feels hollow. Their whispers and side glances are like knives, cutting into me deeper than any physical injury. I know they mean well, but the tension is getting to me.

"You're gonna be fine," Nate says, but even he looks like he's not so sure.

I aim for humor to lighten the mood. "Trying to get rid of me already?"

"Never," he says with a laugh, but his eyes say maybe. Nate is our best batter and a genuinely nice guy. He heads off toward his locker, leaving me standing alone in the middle of the room.

I sit down, pretending to go through my routine. The weights above my locker mock me—packed boxes without a place to land yet. I haven't seen Amy since our workout session yesterday. She has a life outside coaching me, I'm sure, so I couldn't reasonably expect her to be here the moment I arrived for the game.

I rub my shoulder, feeling the dull ache spreading into my chest. But it feels like phantom pain, like I'm talking myself into it.

Amy knocks on the locker-room door. "May I come in?"

"Yep. Nobody's here but me and my trade rumors."

She walks in, hesitating halfway to me. Then she marches straight up to me and sits down beside me. "Charlie, don't let them mess with your head. Trade rumors are just that—gossip."

"Seb heard about it quick like he always does. And he's usually right."

"It's not a done deal," she insists. "We have time."

But does she really know that? Amy is standing right in front of me, shoulder to shoulder, like she's ready to fight this battle for me, with me. I want to believe her, but seeing her here only reminds me of what I stand to lose. It's not just my career on the line—it's everything we started rebuilding between us.

"I should handle this myself, Coach."

"Come on, Charlie, we both know I'm more than your coach." Amy clasps my hands, something I've never seen her do before. "I care about you. A lot."

"I feel that way about you too."

"Good." She stands up, still holding my hands, and waits until I get up too. Then she smiles. "Now, forget about the trade rumor. We have the rest of today and all weekend to explore Cooperstown. I don't want to see any more frowns or bummed-out looks. Let's go to your place and grab whatever you'll need for the weekend."

"Amy, I should be practicing for—"

"No arguments," she declares. "If I see a baseball in your hand before Sunday, the trip is off."

I grin. "You're amazing, Amy."

She winks and guides me out of the locker room. I shove thoughts of trades and defeats behind us. Maybe this will be our last trip together if Philly seals the deal. It might also be the break I need to clear my head. When she's not watching, I catch myself rubbing my shoulder again.

We drive in near silence until we hit traffic.

"Want to talk about it?" she finally asks.

I try to understand the look in her eyes. It's not pity. She wouldn't do that to me. So I tell her, "Just thinking. Philly might want to take me on, but that's only if my injury is healed enough."

"Relax. Your shoulder will be fine."

She squeezes my thigh reassuringly. The way she's acting, I'd almost think she'll pack everything up and bolt with me if I get traded tomorrow.

When we arrive at my apartment, I don't even pretend to pack. Amy sees right through me but keeps up her determined hustle anyway and fixes me with a teasing glare. "You're going to spend all weekend looking like you got traded to the worst team in the league."

I can't help it. I laugh. "But isn't that exactly what…" She cuts me off with two fingers, sealing my lips. "Don't say it. No negative thoughts allowed this weekend. Remember?"

"Right, because you're just so laid back and easygoing."

"You bet I am." Amy sets down an armload of clothes I never intended to wear and ticks off the contents on her fingers. "Toothbrush, check. Warm jacket, check. Goofy smile for photos we're going to take at the museum? Double-check."

"You are singular and amazing, Amy Keller."

She stops rushing around and looks at me like she's seeing something deep inside, a truth about us that even I can't quite put into words yet. Then she nods and smiles, like we've reached an understanding that doesn't require either of us to speak another word. We leave my overstuffed suitcase sprawled open on the floor and jump in the car, craving spontaneity the way only two people living on a ticking clock can. We drive north, letting go of everything except the road ahead, and make it to Cooperstown by midmorning.

The first thing we do is find a room at a quaint little bed-and-breakfast. A cheerful older lady greets us and asks if we need one room or two. Before I realize what I've said, I'm telling her, "One room."

Amy's brows shoot up, but her lips curl into a sweet little smile.

Our hostess leads us upstairs to a beautifully decorated room that has all the charms of upstate New York. How have I never been to Cooperstown before? It's a travesty.

After breakfast, Amy announces it's time to explore America's Hometown, the nickname for Cooperstown. It boasts less than two thousand residents, but the little village houses the Baseball Hall of Fame. Amy insists on driving because she wants me to gaze out at the scenery instead of watching for other drivers. But soon, she finds a good parking spot, and we switch to walking down Main Street to reach the Hall instead.

The adrenaline rush of being here in this place—all baseball, all the time—lights something inside me. I could live in this town for a summer and whisper sweet nothings to the stadium grass if they'd let me camp out at Doubleday Field. When I tell Amy that, she grins and kisses my cheek. Her gentle laughter makes my chest ache in a good way. We take photos next to sculptures and case displays. She stops in front of the "Women in Baseball" exhibit.

It's inspiring to see all the women who once made history, but I only have eyes for one girl.

"We should add you to this display," I joke.

"No thanks. I prefer coaching."

After an amazing lunch at a baseball-themed diner—complete with chocolate-covered waffle cones—we head back to our bed-and-breakfast to regroup. Amy insists on strolling hand-in-hand along the lake until we need to wear our jackets. The air has become crisp and cool, but I like that. It's refreshing. We head back to our room before dinner, and she pulls a bottle of wine out of her bag.

"Glasses?" she asks.

I pop open the bottle with her keychain corkscrew. "We'll improvise."

She pours us each a generous portion in big ceramic mugs that says "Cooperstown or Bust!" We sit wordlessly on the bed, and I watch her sip her drink delicately as she studies me with a tender gaze.

"Charlie, can I ask you something?"

"Of course you can. Go on, ask away."

Amy scuttles closer to me on the bed. "What would make you happy? Really, truly happy?"

Chapter Fifteen
Recommitment

Amy just asked me what amounts to the question of the century, in my mind, and my whole body and brain have become immobilized solely because she wants to know my deepest secret. I don't want to overthink it. So instead, I'm immobilized. Snap out of it, moron. You know what you want and need to tell her. Yeah, I do know. It's ridiculously simple.

"I'm happiest when I'm with you, Amy."

"That's sweet, Charlie." Her tone is firm but also gentle, which somehow makes sense. "I meant not just right now, or just this weekend—but what do you really want deep in your soul?"

I can't help chuckling softly. "Only a woman would talk about my soul. Guys aren't into all that mushy stuff."

"Cut the crap and answer my question."

Her serious expression forces me into an honest response. "What do I want? To play without fear. To chase glory like I used to back when I was the fastball king."

She leans against my shoulder. "I believe you will get there, sooner than you think. I believe that more than ever now."

The warmth of her breath on my neck makes me shiver just a little, and the intimacy of that sensation overwhelms me. I need to tell Amy the truth about what I've known for a while. "Can I ask you something?"

"Only fair to let you interrogate me too."

I take a cleansing breath and go for it. "Would you really stick with me if Philly takes this deal? Or if I get sent down to the minors?"

"You'll have a hard time getting rid of me, Braddock."

I pull her close, the scent of her soothing my angst. "Don't want to get rid of you, baby. In fact, I have plans for us tonight and tomorrow."

"That sounds intriguing." She wraps her arms around my neck. "What's on tap for tonight?"

"Sex, sex, and more sex. Not very original, I know. But I guarantee you won't be disappointed."

I make good on my promise, or "phase one of tonight's agenda," as Amy jokingly calls it. We peel each other's clothes off gradually, ramping up our bedroom adventures until they've become an erotic evening like nothing either of us has done before. I'm hard in record time. The sweet, earthy aroma of Amy's desire for me wafts in the air, turning me on even more. I lay her down on the slippery-soft sheets, her body spread out before me like a Renaissance painting come to life.

She drags her tongue across her lips in leisurely fashion, arching her back just enough to accentuate her tits. "I need you inside me now, Charlie."

"Your wish is my command." I roll on a condom and take a moment purely to admire her incredible body, raking my gaze over her flat abdomen. Then I brush my hands over her silky-smooth skin. I keep going down, down, down, teasing her with the tips of my fingers until I reach the velvety, wet folds between her thighs. When I slide two fingers inside her, she arches her back and moans.

"Charlie, please."

"I want to tease you until you can't stand it anymore, and then you'll beg me to do it again."

"Mm, that sounds wonderful."

I'd hidden a few items under the bed while she was in the bathroom. Now, I will unveil them one by one. First, I pull out a smooth knit scarf that feels almost like silk. "Mind if I tie you to the bed?"

"Anything you want, I want."

I bind her wrists just loose enough that they won't chafe but tight enough she can't control the situation. Then I get to work teasing Amy in earnest while she's restrained, unable to touch me, unable to push me away. I lick a path up her neck, trailing featherlight kisses down to her collarbone. She gasps when I trace my tongue over the swell of her breast, circling around her nipple but never quite reaching it.

"Charlie," she breathes, arching her back.

"Patience," I whisper against her skin.

As I resume my journey down her body, my gaze stays locked on her beautiful eyes, now darkened with desire. I spread her thighs with my knee, then I gently part them even more with my hands. At last, I reach her mound—where all her downy, curly hairs await me. Can't wait to taste her. When I glance up, I find her watching me while her breasts heave with every labored breath. I maintain eye contact as I lower my mouth to her core, savoring her first gasp of pleasure as I suckle her clit. She tastes like heaven—sweet and tangy and uniquely Amy. While I work her with my tongue, I alternate between firm strokes and gentle flicks that make her hips buck against the mattress.

Her legs tremble. Her moans grow louder and more desperate with every passing second.

"Oh god, Charlie, right there," she gasps when I hit a particularly sensitive spot. "Please don't stop, not ever."

Her impassioned plea spurs me to double down, focusing all my attention on her gratification. Amy's thighs clench around my head as she climbs toward her peak inch by inch while she begins to thrash wildly. Her cream covers my face, and the aroma spurs me to push deeper between her folds, grunting with hunger as I devour her, lapping up every last bit of her cream. Amy clasps the scarf tighter, her eyes now squeezed shut and her whimpering cries filling the room.

When she comes, it's with my name on her lips, her body shuddering beneath my touch. It's the most beautiful thing I've ever seen—Amy Keller completely undone, completely vulnerable, completely mine.

Yes, she is mine. Her body, her pleasure, all of it belongs to me.

I crawl up her body, kissing my way back to her lips. She must taste herself on my tongue, but she clearly doesn't mind. My mouth silences her subtle moans.

"I need to feel your big, hard cock buried deep inside me, Charlie. But first, please let me taste you."

"Never can resist anything you want, baby."

I rise to a kneeling position, waddling forward until my erection is waving above her face. Clasping my dick in one hand, I use the other to hold myself up and position the head of my dick directly over her mouth. Then I bend my straight arm just enough that the head grazes her lips and a bead of my cum lies poised on the very tip.

"Devour me, Amy." The deeper, rougher tone in my voice astounds me.

The woman I adore laps up the drop of cum as if she wants to do nothing else for hours on end. She curls her tongue around me again and again. When she wraps her mouth around me fully, she takes me deep inside, her velvety tongue driving me mad. Even with her hands bound, she's in complete control—of me, of my pleasure, of everything. I've surrendered to her willingly. I observe her movements, mesmerized, as she draws me deeper into her mouth, her eyes locked on mine all the while.

"Fuck, Amy," I grunt, thrusting my fingers into her hair. "You're so goddamn beautiful like this."

She hums around me, the vibration sending sparks up my spine. I rock my hips gently, careful not to go too deep, but Amy seems determined to test her limits. Her tongue traces the underside of my cock, finding that sensitive spot just beneath the head that makes me splutter and shout.

"If you keep that up, this will be over way too soon," I warn, but my voice doesn't sound like me anymore. I've become a wild, ravenous beast. Amy is my prey.

She releases me abruptly, licking her lips. "Maybe we should move on to the main event."

I untie her wrists and flip her onto her stomach in one swift movement. She gasps, then moans again as I paint hot kisses down her spine. When I grip her hips, I lift them slightly to position myself behind her. "Is this okay?"

"More than okay." She twists her head around to glance over her shoulder at me. Her lips have deepened to a sexy shade of rose. "I want to feel you everywhere, Amy."

"Yes, I want that too."

I plunge inside her slowly, savoring every inch of her silken heat as it envelops me, and I gently settle my weight atop her. The warmth of her skin and the closeness of our bodies is almost overwhelming. Damn, it's better than any strikeout or even the most perfect pitch. No stadium ovation I've ever experienced could top this. My connection with Amy transcends the physical; it's something deeper, something that makes my chest ache.

The wet sucking sound that accompanies our lovemaking gets me even more turned on. But it's the feel of her silky hair brushing over my skin that seals the deal. I need to take her now, hard, as if my life depends on my ability to fuck her into oblivion. With my body still lying atop hers, I begin to pump my hips. At first, I move in an easy rhythm to let her get used to being fucked from behind, flat on her stomach. But I can't wait long.

Soon, my desperation to come inside her beautiful body seizes me like a black hole sucking me in. Can't think. Can't control my lust. The sucking sound intensifies along with the creaking of the bed frame. My grunts and snarls mingle with Amy's passionate cries. Her nails rake across the sheets.

"Yes, Charlie, oh god, yes! Bang me like a gong!"

Not sure what that means, but I'll do my best.

I thrust harder, deeper, my body slick with sweat as I drive us both toward climax. Amy's moans escalate into sharp cries, growing more frantic, and I can feel her sleek inner muscles tightening around me. The pressure builds at the base of my spine, a telltale sign of an impending explosion.

"Come with me, baby," I growl into her ear, reaching beneath her to grind her clit with my fingers. "Let go—right now."

Her body convulses beneath me in rhythmic pulses. That's all it takes to hurl me over the edge. I bury myself to the hilt and let go, pleasure crashing through me in waves as I empty myself inside her. For a moment, the world narrows to one thing—only us, connected, breathing hard, hearts pounding almost as if we've become one.

I collapse beside Amy, tugging her against my chest. We lie here in silence, our limbs tangled, her breaths warm against my neck. I trace lazy patterns on her back, savoring the softness of her skin under my fingertips. The sex was incredible, but this moment—this quiet intimacy—feels even more significant somehow.

Every time I think we've reached the most important moment in our relationship, I'm proved wrong again. And I can't hold back anymore. I need to speak the words.

"Amy, I'm in love with you."

Chapter Sixteen

The Charity Game

Today is the annual charity game, and I should be focused on that. But my mind keeps rewinding to that night in Cooperstown, and how Amy responded after I told her I'm in love with her. She stared blankly at me for so long that I almost thought I'd abruptly lost my hearing. But no, that wasn't what happened.

"Did you hear me, Amy? I said—"

"I'm exhausted, Charlie. Let's go to sleep."

With that, she flipped over onto her side, effectively ending the conversation. In the morning, the situation did not improve. Ever since, she's been all business—talking to me like I'm a rookie in a slump instead of her, ah…boyfriend? That term doesn't seem appropriate. Amy isn't in the bullpen, but I assume she will show up. She's my coach, after all.

Don't think about her. Focus on the game.

As if my girl problems weren't enough, the Admirals will be facing off against the Altitude once again. I'm not exactly thrilled by the prospect of meeting up with my old buddy Jared Morris. But I'm determined to exact my revenge on that dickwad once and for all. Okay, a charity match might not be the best time. But I absolutely need to whup his ass in monumental fashion.

Morris is going down hard this time.

The charity game is about to start, and I'm standing in the bullpen, trying to focus on my warm-up pitches. But Amy's voice keeps cutting through my concentration as she discusses strategy with Coach Rivera nearby.

"His fastball's looking good today," Amy announces, not even glancing my way. "Let's see if he can maintain that control for two full innings."

Her statement stings more than I would've expected. Not because she said something critical, but because of how detached she sounded. Like I'm just another project for her, not the guy who bared his soul back in Cooperstown.

I wind up and fire another pitch, harder than necessary. The bullpen catcher's mitt smacks loudly.

"Easy, Braddock," Dave Lawrence calls. "Save some for the actual game."

"Sorry. Guess I'm picturing Jared Morris's face instead of a catcher's mitt."

The stadium is full today, buzzing with energy beyond these walls. Kids from the local youth programs are getting tours of the dugout, and that's what this is all about. I need to remember my personal drama with Amy and my beef with Morris aren't the objective today.

"Two minutes, Braddock," Coach Rivera reminds us.

I nod, taking a deep breath as I prepare for my final warm-up pitch. The ball flies out of my hand with perfect rotation, hitting the catcher's mitt dead center.

Amy almost smiles, finally acknowledging I exist—sort of. "That's what I like to see."

Her gaze holds mine for a second. Whatever it was, it vanishes in a flash as she turns away. "Remember your mechanics. Don't over-throw."

"Got it, Coach." Emphasizing her title didn't phase her at all. *Rats.*

When I step onto the field, the crowd's reaction is mixed—some cheers, some skeptical murmurs. They've all heard about my injury and my struggles. I survey the crowd briefly before focusing on the mound. The familiar dirt beneath my cleats grounds me. This is where I belong.

Then I see him, and my jaw tightens.

Jared Morris is warming up in the opposite dugout. When he notices me, he smirks while pantomiming a throwing motion that mocks my injury. Then he taps his shoulder with exaggerated concern.

"Feeling fragile today, Braddock?" He kept his words hushed, but I heard his snide remark.

I shake my head and turn away, refusing to take the bait. Not today. Not when there are scouts in the stands and kids looking up to us.

Not when Amy is watching.

The first batter steps up to the plate—some Altitude rookie I don't recognize. I get the sign from the catcher and nod. The weight of the ball feels perfect in my hand. I wind up, channeling all the frustration of the past few weeks into my mechanics, not my velocity. The pitch flies true, right at the corner of the strike zone. The rookie's eyes widen a fraction before he swings late, missing by inches.

"Strike one!"

A murmur ripples through the crowd. I don't react, keeping my face neutral despite the satisfaction warming my chest. The catcher tosses the ball back, and I roll it between my fingers, finding the seams.

Just like Amy taught me.

Two more pitches and the rookie is walking back to the dugout, shaking his head. One down.

"You're on fire, Braddock," someone shouts from our dugout. I don't turn to see who it is, but it sounds like Dante Roberts.

The next batter steps up, a veteran I've faced before. He fouls off my first pitch, then watches the second sail by for a strike. On the third, he makes contact—a sharp grounder that our shortstop scoops up effortlessly before firing to first. Two down.

I glance toward our dugout, catching Amy's gaze briefly. She gives me a small nod—the closest thing to approval I've seen from her in days. It shouldn't mean as much as it does.

The third batter is Morris himself, of course. This time, I'm ready for whatever he throws at me. He swaggers up to the plate, tapping his bat against his cleats before settling into his stance. His eyes zero in on mine in a deliberate challenge.

"How's the arm, Braddock?" he stage-whispers to make sure no one else hears. "Ready to embarrass yourself?"

I won't respond to his ridicule. He'd love that. Instead, I take my time finding the perfect grip. The stadium seems to quiet around us as I wind up, my motion smooth and controlled—exactly how Amy and I practiced it a hundred times. The ball rockets out of my hand, hurtling through the air with purpose. It's not my fastest pitch, but it is my most precise—a fastball with just enough movement to catch the inside corner.

Jared's eyes widen for a split second before he swings. Too late. The satisfying smack of the ball hitting the catcher's mitt is followed by the umpire's call.

"Strike one!"

The crowd responds with scattered applause, growing louder as they realize what they're seeing. I'm back. Maybe not at full strength yet, but yeah, I am definitely back.

Morris steps out of the box, adjusting his gloves with a scowl. He mutters, "Lucky pitch."

I ignore him and, instead, focus on my breathing. Amy taught me how to do that during those long rehab sessions. In through the nose, out through the mouth. Center yourself. Find your balance.

The next pitch comes in a bit faster. Morris fouls it off, the ball skipping toward our dugout.

"Getting warmed up?" he says mockingly as the catcher tosses me a new ball.

I roll my shoulders and focus. The third pitch is my slider—the one that's given me the most trouble during rehab. Amy watches me intently, analyzing every movement of my delivery. The ball breaks late, diving away from Jared's bat as he swings through empty air.

"Strike three! You're out!"

The crowd erupts. Three up, three down. I walk off the mound, keeping my expression neutral despite the fire in my veins.

I did it. Holy shit, I did it! First inning back, and I struck out Jared Effing Morris. Okay "Effing" isn't his actual middle name. But it should be. I just can't say "Jared Fucking Morris" in polite company.

When I reach the dugout, the team greets me with fist bumps and shoulder slaps. But it's Amy I'm searching for in the crowd. She's standing slightly apart from the others, her expression guarded but her eyes saying something else entirely.

"Good control out there," she states like a true professional coach. "Your mechanics held up well."

"Thanks to you," I say, and I mean it sincerely.

As she hands me a water bottle, our fingers brush against each other, and for a split second, her professional mask slips. I glimpse the woman from Cooperstown, the one who laughed with me over beers and challenged me to stupid bar games. The one who kissed me back with all her heart and soul. The woman I made love to in that bed-and-breakfast.

Then she's gone, replaced by Coach Keller once more.

"Stay loose for your second inning," she advises, moving away. "And watch Morris in the box. He'll be looking to get even."

I gulp down a long drink of water, watching her walk to the far end of the dugout. Coach Rivera slides up next to me, his weathered face cracking into a rare smile.

"That's how you shut up a loudmouth," he says, slapping my shoulder. "Damn fine pitching, son."

"Thanks, Coach." Though I spoke those words, I'm hung up on watching Amy as she studies her clipboard.

Rivera isn't my coach, but Amy hasn't minded taking advice from him. Nobody could be angry about that. Adrian Rivera is the nicest guy on the planet—who can be tough as hell when necessary.

The Admirals are up to bat now, and I should be focusing on our offense, but my mind is still processing what just happened on the mound. Not just striking out Jared, but the way my shoulder felt. Strong. Reliable. Like I can trust it again. But I know I shouldn't expect my shoulder to be one hundred percent healed today. I'll still have bad moments, though I'm sure those times will be fewer and farther between.

When it's time for my second inning, I roll my shoulders and grab my glove. As I walk back to the mound, I catch sight of a familiar face in the stands—Alicia. My ex-wife is sitting behind home plate, probably analyzing every pitch for her next article. Yeah, I heard she took a job with a big sports magazine. She'd been a columnist before I ever met her, though only for small publications. She left me for her career, so I hope it's made her happy.

Great. Just what I need. My ex-wife analyzing my every play.

I don't care about that as much as I thought I would. The moment I catch sight of Amy, I forget all about Alicia and Jared.

I'll win this game for the woman I love, whether she likes it or not.

Chapter Seventeen
Showdown with Jared

A charity game designed to raise money for sick children probably isn't the right time to face down against Jared. That jerk has been acting like he owns the diamond and the stands and all the fans who've come here for some fun. I'm standing on the mound, preparing to throw another wicked pitch, when I spot Amy in the bullpen again.

She's not looking at me, but I can feel her presence like a steadying hand on my shoulder. Her clipboard is clutched tight against her chest as if she's counting every pitch. Even from here, I can see her lips moving silently, running through strategy or maybe just willing me to kick Jared's ass.

I roll the baseball between my fingers, feeling the familiar seams. This isn't about Jared right now, though. It's about these kids watching from the stands, some in wheelchairs, others with IV poles. They're the real MVPs today.

"Just throw the damn ball already, Braddock!" Morris shouts from the opposing dugout. "Those kids wanna see some action before their next hospital visit!"

My grip tightens on the ball. A flush of heat crawls up my neck, and for a split second, I consider firing the ball at Morris instead of the plate.

But I catch Amy's eye, and she shakes her head almost imperceptibly. Message received.

Then a little boy—maybe six years old—comes barreling out of the dugout. He's grinning and waving at me, shouting something that I can't quite make out. Amy sprints after him wearing a sheepish grin.

The little guy flings his arms around my waist and grins up at me. "Charlie Braddock. You're my favorite player of all time."

"Wow, that's quite a compliment." I ruffle the kid's hair. "What's your name, buddy?"

"August Murphy."

"Did you come here on your own?"

He shakes his head. "My mom and dad are in the dugout. It's so cool that I get to watch you play. Mostly, I'm stuck at home 'cause I've got cancer. It's in my brain."

My throat constricts. This adorable kid loves me. He ran out here just to meet me, despite his illness. He's amazing. And I need to do something for my biggest fan, don't I? So, I sweep August up in my arms.

A woman rushes over to us, panting from exertion while also smiling. "Mr. Braddock, I'm sorry August surprised you that way, but he really does worship you. I'm Jill Murphy, August's mom. My husband is saving our seats for us. I hope our boy didn't mess up your pitch."

"No, not at all. Any kid as brave as August deserves a little something special." I bend forward until my head touches his. "How would you like to throw a pitch with me? All your friends will be super jealous."

August grins again. "Please, please! Let's do it!"

With the kid in my arms, we both wind our arms back together, his small hand nestled inside mine. The ball feels right between our shared grip. The crowd goes wild as we launch the ball toward the plate—not the fastest pitch of my career, but definitely the most meaningful.

"Strike!" the umpire calls, playing along perfectly. He even waves at August.

The kid erupts into cheers, bouncing in my arms. "We did it! We threw a strike! Can't wait to tell Dad about it."

Now the entire stadium is on their feet, clapping and cheering—even some of the opposing team. Everyone except Jared, that is, who leans against the dugout rail with a sour expression. Guess that jackoff won't give up his hatred of me even for a kid with cancer.

"That's my boy," August's mother says, tears glistening in her eyes as I set him down. She whispers to me, "Thank you."

I wink—and she kisses my cheek. In a chaste way, naturally.

Amy leads August and his mom back to the dugout, but not before giving me a look that makes my heart skip. Pride, warmth, and something deeper that I can't quite name. It's almost like she's seeing a different side of me—not just the pitcher with a wicked fastball, but something more.

When I turn back to the mound, I'm suddenly laser focused thanks to August Murphy. I'll win this game for him. The crowd noise fades to a distant hum as I glance toward Morris, who's now pacing in the opposite dugout. For once, his taunts can't penetrate my concentration.

My next pitch is a screamer. The batter doesn't even swing—just watches it sail past.

"Strike one!" The umpire's call rings clear across the diamond.

I catch the return throw, roll my shoulders, and reset. August is watching from the dugout, his small face pressed against the chain link. I'm not just throwing for me anymore. I'm throwing for him, for all these kids who need heroes to believe in.

Jared gives an exaggerated eye roll.

Oh, I want to pitch the ball straight at his smug face instead of the plate. Yeah, okay, I won't kick Jared in the balls—today.

I turn back to the batter. The kid's maybe eighteen, wearing an Admirals jersey that hangs off his thin frame. His arms look like twigs, but his eyes are fierce with determination.

"You got this," I mouth to him, nodding encouragingly.

Then I wind up and deliver a pitch with just enough speed to challenge the kid without overwhelming him. He connects with a solid crack that sends the ball sailing over the shortstop's head. The crowd erupts as he takes off running, his face split with a grin so wide it must hurt.

"That's it! Go, go, go!" I find myself shouting, pumping my fist as he rounds first base.

Amy gives me a thumbs-up sign and mouths, "Fastball fever!"

Her expression is filled with…love.

And suddenly, I feel ten feet tall. I'm not just Charlie Braddock, struggling pitcher trying to make a comeback. I'm August's hero. And maybe, just maybe, I'm worthy of that look Amy just gave me.

Another batter approaches the plate. I wind up again and deliver a fastball that sings through the air, popping into the catcher's mitt with a satisfying thwack.

"Strike one!"

The crowd roars. I can pick out August's voice among them, squealing with delight. I glance at the radar gun: 98 mph. Not bad for a charity game.

"Lucky pitch," Jared calls from the dugout. "Let's see you do it again, has-been!"

I ignore him, focusing on the feel of the ball in my hand, the weight of it against my fingertips. The seams are perfect ridges beneath my skin. The smell of freshly cut grass, the hot dogs from the concession stand, and the faint scent of chalk from the baselines grounds me to this moment.

My next pitch is even faster. The batter swings—a second too late.

"Strike two!"

The crowd is on their feet now. I can see August jumping up and down, his small hands pumping the air. His parents are beaming, their arms around each other, watching their son experience pure joy. For a moment, I forget about my failed marriage, about Alicia leaving, about all the nights I spent wondering if I'd ever find my way back to the mound.

This moment—right here—this is what matters.

I wind up for the final pitch, feeling the energy of the stadium wrap around me like a warm embrace. The batter sets his jaw, determined not to strike out. I respect that fight. I deliver a changeup that seems to hang in the air for an eternity before dropping like a stone just as he swings. The bat whooshes through empty space.

"Strike three! You're out!"

The stadium erupts. I pump my fist, allowing myself a moment of pure, unfiltered celebration. My gaze finds Amy first—always Amy—and she's beaming at me with those expressive eyes that see right through my defenses.

When I jog back to the dugout, August high-fives me with such enthusiasm that I worry he might hurt his small hand.

"That was awesome!" He's practically vibrating with excitement. "Can you teach me how to throw like that?"

"Sure thing, buddy."

"You've got the fastest fastball ever!"

I chuckle. "Not quite. But I'm aiming for it."

Jared stalks up to me, fuming so hard I swear steam is rolling out of his ears. "You might've beaten our team, but you aren't the fastball king anymore. Those pitches were practically softballs."

"Go suck a lemon, Morris. Nobody cares about the outcome of a charity game."

He snorts. "Oh, this wasn't about winning for myself. It was about showing everyone that you're washed up, Braddock. Your shoulder's shot, and we both know it."

I grind my teeth so hard I half expect them to crack. The worst part is that on my darkest days, I've had the same thoughts. But today isn't one of those days. I know Jared is full of shit, but I won't argue with him now. "Don't spoil it for the kids, hey, Morris? This is their day, not ours."

"Charlie!" August tugs at my uniform. "Don't listen to that mean man. You're the best pitcher in the whole wide world!"

Something loosens in my chest at the kid's unwavering faith. I ruffle his hair again and bend down to his level. "Thanks, buddy. That means a lot coming from you."

When I straighten up, Amy is there, positioning herself subtly between me and Morris. "Great pitching today, Charlie."

She said that loud enough for everyone to hear.

The color commentator informs everyone in the stadium that it's time for the players to meet with the children. I'm looking forward to that, and August will be my guide. He really is the sweetest kid. Once all the players have left the field, August waves for me to follow his family.

But Amy is jogging up to me, so I call out to the kid, "Be there in a few minutes, buddy!"

She halts only a foot away from me. For what feels like forever, she stares at me as if she doesn't know what to say now. I'm about to open my mouth when she finally speaks.

"I'm in love with you too, Charlie."

My grin must look stupid, but I don't give a hoot. I drag Amy into my arms and kiss her like there's no one else in the entire world except the two of us.

Chapter Eighteen
Clearing the Air

We sit across from each other, a bottle of wine between us and the city lights playing off the river outside the window. The bar is warm and intimate, the opposite of what I'm used to lately thanks to my life on the road. Amy goes with me to every game. But since players usually don't get more than one day off every ten days, she mostly serves as my coach—not my girlfriend.

Well, except at night. She's my girl all the way when we're under the covers together. I lean toward Amy. "I couldn't have won that game this evening without you."

Amy looks like a different person, out of her element in this romantic setting. She probably wouldn't like it if I said so, but she seems more feminine in the subdued lighting. I love her tough-coach side too, don't get me wrong. She must think I look like a waiter, with my tie and spiffy slacks. I feel a little off tonight, probably because it's been at least five hours since my coach yelled at me to hustle. She hasn't called me Braddock either.

I can't remember the last time I talked with someone instead of getting talked at. Hence, our private dinner.

"Finally realized I'm not the enemy, huh?" she says, one corner of her mouth curling up. She tilts her head, studying me, the edge of a grin still playing at her lips.

"I'm reserving judgment." I say with a straight face.

She lets out a small, genuine laugh.

To see her like this, as lovely as an angel from heaven—it takes my breath away. I glance at the big picture windows, my gaze roving the entire dimly lit room. I feel a bit uncertain now that I can't just hide behind my usual dumb jokes. I try to relax into the chair and ignore the nagging instinct that this silence needs to be filled with stats and strategy.

"Things were rough for a while," I admit. "Losing nine games in a row? I felt like I was stranded in the middle of the ocean with no life preserver, about to sink into the depths. Nothing worked. I was swinging at air." My fingers drum lightly on the table. "You sure as hell turned me around, though."

"I told you individual practice would fire up your fastball in no time." She slides a hand onto my thigh under the table. "But it was the pitching drills, customized warm-up routines, and specialized strength and conditioning that turned the tide."

"Easy, baby. Get me too worked up under the table, and I might fuck you in front of all these high-toned diners."

She moves her hand up to my groin.

I cough into my fist.

As I pick up my glass, the stem feels cool in my hand. I'm buying a moment to gather the words I need to tell her what I want. The kind of words that don't come easy. I can feel her watching me, waiting. "I can get awfully caught up in the game—in winning. Alicia always complained about that. She wouldn't even go to home games to watch me play."

"You think you're the only one who gets too caught up?" Her voice has an edge in it, a challenge, but she doesn't back off. "I've always felt I'm chasing my father's shadow." She gazes past me, into someplace I can't see. "He was a legend. I feel like I have to live up to that."

"I get that. It can be hard to live up to a legend. Wanting to succeed for someone else can be a huge weight." I take a sip of wine, then delicately swirl my finger in circles. "My grandfather was a huge baseball fan. He took me to games as often as possible, and Granddad's love of baseball inspired my love of the sport. Unfortunately, he died before I worked my way up to the majors."

"I'm sure he's watching you, somehow, some way." She rubs her cheek against mine. "The ones we've lost motivate us to be more than we thought we could be."

While Amy and I sip from our glasses, the alcohol warming our veins, I begin to wonder if wanting something is enough to make it happen. She's quiet, her fingers idly tracing the rim of her glass, the set of her shoulders a little looser now. I can't remember ever seeing her this relaxed, and I hope this mood won't fade away too soon.

"Did you have someone to cheer you on while you chased your dreams?" I ask. "Or just guys like me making your life hell?"

"My mother has been my biggest fan and my best friend." Her voice is hushed now, and her eyes have turned softer too. "She's supportive, but…since my dad passed, it's been just the two of us. No brothers or sisters, just me and Mom."

"Two women on their own. Must've been tough growing up that way."

"More like one woman trying to keep up with her tomboy daughter," she corrects, a hint of a smile ghosting over her lips. "How about you? All baseball, all the time?"

"Yeah, pretty much. It's always pulsed through my veins." I smile slightly as I remember my childhood. "I had my parents and three sisters to keep me in line."

"Three sisters?" Her smile broadens, and I find myself mirroring it. "That must've been a wild upbringing."

"Nah, not really. Mom and Dad kept us from turning into heathens." A sly grin stretches my lips. "But I found lots of ways to harass my sisters. They harassed me right back."

Amy laughs delicately. "Wish I'd known you then. We would've gotten along like peas in a pod."

This is what it means to be off the field, truly off the field, and away from the pressure of games and reporters. "You should meet them. My family, I mean. You could see how a big family does things."

"Yeah?" She seems caught off guard, the hesitation making her appear younger as she draws out the solitary word.

"Three sisters, two parents, lots of chaos. It's a little different from what you're used to."

I expect her to say something cutting, but the vulnerable admission has stuck, and for once, she lets it. "We'll see."

A companionable silence settles over us. I don't think I've been this open, this honest, with anyone in a long time. It makes me uneasy and peaceful at the same time.

"Charlie Braddock," someone says. That voice interrupts us, and I turn to see a kid of maybe seventeen. He's barely holding back his excitement. There's a small group at their table, shifting awkwardly, not sure how to start whatever it is they want to do.

A couple guys in baseball caps and a couple women with eager, open expressions approach us. Fans, unmistakably. The Jacksonville type that made the trip all the way here. It's always a shock to see them when I'm not wearing my uniform, like someone is catching me in a lie. They hover nearby but not too near, seemingly undecided about whether to talk to me or Amy.

I smile, the expression a little lopsided, aiming for reassurance. "Hey, c'mon over here. We don't bite. Usually."

One of the guys pushes a ball cap forward and hesitates. "Would you mind…?"

"Signing?" I finish for him. "Yeah. Sure."

The table is quickly flooded with caps and Sharpies. Amy glances at me, wide-eyed and bemused. I make quick work of the first ball, nodding toward her. "You gotta meet the real star behind my comeback." There's a rush of embarrassment in the group. I can almost hear the collective oh. "This is my coach, Amy Keller."

I watch her, waiting for the reaction. It doesn't disappoint.

"Wow." One of the women elbows the others, then beams at Amy. "You're amazing. Could we have a photo with you, Coach Keller?"

She clearly doesn't know what to say at first. There's something different about being seen like this. "Don't let him fool you. Charlie's the one who does all the work. I just keep him from making an ass of himself."

The ladies giggle and grin.

We both sign the merch piled in front of us. There's a shift in the air, the awkwardness lifting as everyone begins to talk at once. Amy joins in with them, answering questions, quick and confident, a new ease in her movements. She handles herself like she's been doing it all her life.

"Did you really bring Braddock back from the dead?" one of the male fans teases.

"Wasn't easy," Amy throws back. "He's stubborn."

She casts a glance my way, and I wink.

"You're lucky to have her," the youngest one says to me, wide-eyed.

"Don't I know it," I answer, maybe more sincerely than I meant to.

The women are all looking at me with "awwww" eyes. That's what I like to call it. Ladies always love me.

The conversation grows more boisterous as fans talk over each other in a buzz of questions and laughter. I catch Amy's eye across the table. There's a shared feeling between us, an unspoken acknowledgment of what just happened. It feels good.

The group trickles away with waves and promises to cheer us on, leaving us alone again with our drinks. The space they leave behind is warm, less like absence, more like anticipation.

"I think I'm starting to like it when people pester me," Amy says, leaning back and stretching her arms. "As long as they don't ask about RBIs."

"Think you'll be ready for family gatherings pretty soon?"

"I don't know." She lifts her glass, rolling it between her palms. "Will I have to sign autographs at your parents' house too?"

I chuckle. "You never know. My sisters are big fans of the Admirals."

"And they hate the Altitude, right?"

"Got it in one, coach."

The bar grows louder as the night stretches on, glasses clinking and laughter spreading out into the darkness beyond the river. Amy and I agree that we'd rather go home and entertain each other instead of heading to a nightclub. Bedroom play feels like the kind of game I can win. And our last game before the World Series might change the Admirals' fortunes for good—if we can beat Jared Morris and the rest of the Altitude team.

Chapter Nineteen
Season's End

Cheers erupt all around us in a deafening display of team spirit, from the players and the fans. Their sheer joy has infected the stadium. Why? Because for the first time in my career, I'm on the winning team. The Admirals have made it to the summit of baseball. We'll go head-to-head with the Altitude, and by extension, Jared Morris.

This time, I'll be ready for the jackass.

Amy throws her arms around my neck, her feet hovering above the grass. Her exuberant grin spills over into my expression too. "We did it, Charlie! We're going to the World Series!"

My coach kisses me so passionately that I'm wondering when a cop will show up to arrest us for public indecency.

The team swarms around us, laughing and slapping each other on the back. Amy moves out of the way, clearly realizing my teammates want to express their happiness. That means they're now practically tackling me in their fervor.

"You did it, Charlie!" Mike Tanner shouts. Our rookie shortstop has been looking at me like I hung the moon ever since spring training. "That fastball in the eighth? Pure fire, man!"

I laugh, trying to catch my breath as more bodies pile on. "We all did it. Every damn one of us. That's why it's called a team sport."

Our top batter, Dante Roberts, gets in on the action too, smacking my shoulder while laughing. "That breaking ball you taught me saved my butt today. You're the real MVP, Braddock."

The celebration moves from the field to the locker room in a blur of champagne sprays and thunderous music. Someone's blasting "We Are The Champions" at a volume that would make my ears bleed if I wasn't riding so high thanks to adrenaline and victory.

I catch glimpses of Amy through the chaos, her hair damp with champagne, cheeks flushed with excitement as she accepts congratulations from management. Even Phil and Ray are ecstatic. Amy belongs here as much as any of us—more, even. Her father's legacy and dreams live on in her coaching. She's carried his dream forward with a determination that still leaves me in awe.

When Amy's eyes meet mine across the room, everything else fades away. The noise, the crowd, the sticky floor beneath my cleats—it all dissolves into background noise. Her smile, the one reserved just for me, sends a jolt through my system that rivals the adrenaline rush of striking out the final batter.

I weave through the celebrating bodies, dodging champagne streams and ignoring the calls for another toast. When I reach Amy, I don't hesitate. I pull her into a secluded corner of the locker room, away from the cameras and prying eyes.

"We're really doing this," I whisper, my forehead pressed against hers. "The World Series."

Amy's fingers trace the Admirals logo on my champagne-soaked jersey. "Against the Altitude, no less. Poetic, isn't it?"

I groan. "Those assholes have had it coming for years."

"Language, Braddock," she teases, but there's no irritation behind it. We both know exactly what the Altitude means to us. Not just a rival team, but the ones who nearly ended my career last season.

"You know what this means, right?" I trace my thumb along her jawline. "This is our chance to close that chapter for good."

"For the team," she agrees, "but mostly for you. Jared Morris should never have gotten away scot-free after what he did."

"No proof he did it on purpose. But I know he was trying to take me out of commission."

I remember that day as if it happened last night. The fastball that went wild, the collision at home plate, the months of rehab that followed, the doubt that plagued me through every painful step. And all of that happened because of Jared Effing Morris.

"Hey." Amy's voice pulls me back to the present. Her hands frame my face, forcing me to meet her gaze. "You're not the same pitcher you were then. You're better."

Before I can respond, Phil's voice booms through the locker room. "All right, you animals! Management wants everyone cleaned up and presentable for the press conference in thirty minutes. Try not to look like you've been swimming in booze!"

I glance down at my soaked uniform and grin at Amy. "Too late for that."

"Go get changed," she laughs, pushing at my chest. "I'll see you in the press room."

With one last quick kiss, I reluctantly let her go and head to my locker. The guys are still celebrating, but there's purpose in their movements now as they towel off and change into fresh clothes. I strip off my champagne-drenched jersey, tossing it into the laundry hamper before grabbing my shower kit.

Under the hot spray, I close my eyes and let the reality of what we accomplished sink in at last. We're going to the World Series. Against the Altitude. Against Jared Morris. *You are going down, asswipe, going down hard.*

The water sluices away the sticky residue of champagne, but it can't wash away the resolve that's been building inside me since the day I hit the ground at the Altitude's home plate. I've been waiting for this moment—this exact matchup—for so long that I can almost taste it.

As I towel off and pull on my team-issued suit for the press conference, Dante appears beside me, freshly showered and grinning.

"You ready to face Morris again?" he asks, adjusting his tie.

I meet his gaze in the mirror. "More than ready."

"Good, because word is he's already running his mouth about you. Some reporter caught him after the game saying you got lucky with your comeback."

My jaw tightens. "Lucky? I worked my ass off for months."

"We all know that, man." Dante claps my shoulder. "And we'll be right there with you when you shut him up for good."

The press conference is packed when we arrive. Cameras flash like lightning, capturing our sloppy grins for posterity. Phil handles most of the opening statements, talking about team spirit and perseverance, but everyone knows the real story they want.

Me versus Jared Morris.

I'm sitting between Amy and Dante when a reporter finally asks the question hanging in the air.

"Charlie, you'll be facing Jared Morris for the first time since your injury last season," Seb Hudson helpfully reminds me, as if I don't know that already. "Any thoughts about that matchup?"

The room goes quiet. I can feel Amy tense beside me, her hand finding mine under the table and giving it a reassuring squeeze.

"Baseball's a game of second chances," I tell Seb, choosing my words carefully. "I'm grateful to be here with the Admirals, heading to the World Series. That's what matters."

"But Morris has been quoted saying your comeback was more luck than skill, and that facing him again will expose the—"

"I don't concern myself with what Jared Morris thinks," I cut him off, more tersely than I'd intended. "My stats speak for themselves. The Admirals speak for themselves. We've earned this opportunity."

Amy's thumb traces small circles on my hand under the table. It grounds me, keeps me from saying what I really want to about that smug bastard. Jared is the King of Jackassery.

"Will your history with Morris affect your pitching strategy?" another reporter calls out.

I lean forward, making direct eye contact with the camera. "My strategy is the same as it's always been—pitch the best game I can for my team. Nothing else matters."

The questions continue, but I barely register them. I'm going to make Jared Morris eat every arrogant word he's ever spoken about me.

When the press conference finally wraps up, I'm drained but wired at the same time. The team heads out to continue the celebration at our usual spot downtown, but I hang back, needing a moment to process everything.

Amy finds me in the empty hallway outside the press room. She leans against the wall beside me. "You okay, Charlie?"

"Yeah, of course." I run a hand through my still-damp hair. "Just taking time to process that it's really happening. Our team is going all the way. Even if we lose—which I doubt—it'll still be something none of us will ever forget."

"That's true." She nudges me in the side. "But you're thinking about Morris."

I laugh humorlessly. "Am I that transparent?"

"Only to me." She slides an arm around my waist. "The others just see their ace pitcher ready to dominate. I see the guy who spent months in physical therapy to be able to throw again."

I tilt my head to look at her, this woman who's seen me at my lowest and still believes in me. "You know what's crazy? A year ago, I thought facing Morris again would be about revenge. About proving something to him."

"And now?" Amy asks. "How are you feeling? Confident?"

"Yeah, I realize it's about proving something to myself." I tug her closer, craving her warmth and softness. "I'm not defined by that injury anymore. I've become more than just the guy who got taken out by a dirty play. And two weeks from today, I'll get my chance to show the world what a dirty bastard Morris is—and how fast I can pitch these days."

Amy rests her head on my shoulder. "You've already proven that, Charlie. The whole league knows it."

"Maybe." I press a kiss to her temple. "But I need to face him on that mound. I need to look him in the eye when he's at the plate and show him exactly who Charlie Braddock is. I'll wallop him with a pitch so fast he won't be able to see it coming."

"I know you will." Amy smiles sweetly. "You've got fastball fever. We both do."

That magic fastball is waiting for me.

Chapter Twenty
The Playoffs

Two weeks after our glory on the diamond, we step onto the field once again to face off against the Altitude—and specifically Jared Morris. Redemption and revenge all wrapped up in one package. This isn't a charity game. We have arrived at Admirals Stadium in Jacksonville for the first match in the World Series.

We've come home.

The crowd is already on its feet, ready to give their all for the hometown heroes. A sea of jerseys—our jerseys—fills the stands. The rumble of excitement vibrates through the air, through my cleats, straight into my bones.

"Hell of a day for baseball," Phil says, clapping me on the shoulder as we head toward the dugout. He doesn't usually join us there during games, but this is no ordinary matchup.

"Can't wait for the game to start," I tell Phil as I sweep my gaze over the stands. My parents and my sisters are here somewhere, probably wearing those embarrassing shirts with my face plastered on them. And, of course, Amy will be watching from her spot near the bullpen. My heart skips a beat every time I think of that. My girl, the woman I love, will witness my first-ever World Series game.

"Nervous?" Phil asks.

"Nah." I say that, but I feel a bit queasy. "Well, maybe a little."

The locker room buzz still echoes in my head. Jared's smug face is plastered across every sports network this morning as talking heads drone on and on about how they're predicting the Altitude to take it in six games. Some rookie analyst even had the balls to suggest my arm was still questionable. That my injury might flare up under pressure.

"Braddock!"

I turn to see Jared sauntering across the field, doing warm-ups, that trademark smirk on his face. Six months of humility apparently wore off fast once they clinched their playoff spot.

"Ready to embarrass yourself in front of the home crowd?" he says, his voice just loud enough for nearby fans to hear.

I don't take the bait. No, I just smile and continue my stretching routine. Amy taught me that—the power of not engaging, saving my energy for what matters.

"What's wrong, lost your voice along with your fastball?" Jared taunts.

"Save it for the game, Morris," I reply calmly, meeting his gaze. "Talking doesn't win World Series games."

His face hardens, but he huffs and turns away. I can't help but feel a small victory in that. The old Charlie would have fired back, would have let Jared get under my skin until my pitching suffered for it.

"Good man," Phil says with an approving nod, patting my shoulder. "Save the heat for your arm."

The sun beats down on the field as we finish warming up. My arm feels strong, loose, ready. I rotate my shoulder, testing the once-injured joint. No pain, no tightness. Just power waiting to be unleashed.

I spot Amy by the bullpen, clipboard in hand, talking with one of the relief pitchers. She catches my eye and gives me a quick wink before returning to her conversation. That small gesture sends warmth through my chest that has very little to do with the Florida heat.

"Starting lineup, gather 'round!" Phil hollers.

The guys huddle up, and I take my place among them. We're a unit now, bonded through all the ups and downs of the season. I glance at the faces around me, these men who have become family.

"Admirals on three," our captain says, and we all put our hands in the center. "One, two, three—"

"ADMIRALS!" we roar, and the crowd roars back.

As I jog toward the bullpen for final warm-ups, I catch sight of Jared in the visitor's dugout. He's watching me, calculating. I know what he's thinking. He's wondering if I'm the same pitcher he faced last time, or if I've found something new.

The truth is, I have. Something new, stronger, and better.

Amy meets me at the bullpen, her eyes bright with a mix of professional assessment and personal pride. "How does the arm feel?"

"Strong." I flex my fingers around the ball. "Better than ever."

"Remember what we worked on. Don't overthrow. Trust your mechanics."

"Yes, Coach," I say with a smile, and she rolls her eyes.

"Save the sass for after you win."

I take my position on the mound for my warm-up throws, feeling the firmness of the ball, a reassuring sensation. It's familiar, comforting. The catcher signals, and I nod, winding up for the pitch. The ball flies true, smacking into his mitt with a satisfying pop.

"That's what I call a perfect pitch, Braddock!" someone yells from the stands.

Six months ago, I was afraid my career might be over, and I wasn't sure if I'd ever throw a fastball over ninety again. Now I'm opening Game One of the World Series against the team that tried to break me.

The warm-up pitches feel like butter—smooth, controlled, powerful. Each throw builds my confidence. I'm in the zone, that perfect mental space where nothing exists but the ball, the glove, and the space between them.

"Two minutes," the umpire calls.

I scan the stadium one more time. The roar of the crowd washes over me like a wave. This is what I've worked for. This is why I pushed through the pain, the doubt, the endless physical therapy sessions.

Amy gives me a final nod from her position. There's so much in that simple gesture—pride, faith, love. I nod back, a silent promise passing between us. I won't let her down. Not today. Not ever. Everything is on the line tonight.

An announcement booms through the stadium: "Ladies and gentlemen, please rise for our national anthem."

I remove my cap and hold it over my heart, staring at the massive flag unfurling across the outfield. The singer's voice soars through the stadium, and for a moment, everything else fades away. It's just me, the field, and this perfect moment of anticipation and pride in my country.

When the anthem ends, the crowd erupts. I retake my spot on the mound as our play-by-play announcer's voice thunders through the speakers. "And now, taking the mound for your Jacksonville Admirals, number thirty-four, Chaaaaaarlie Braddock!"

The roar is deafening. I tip my cap to the crowd, to my parents, to Amy, to her mom, and then lock in. Game face on. The home plate umpire signals, and the first Altitude batter strides to the plate.

Jared's the leadoff hitter, of course. A wiry speedster who's stolen thirty bases this season.

I breathe deeply through my nostrils, letting the weight of the ball ground me. The seams press against my fingertips as I grip my four-seam fastball. The catcher flashes the sign—fastball, inside corner. I nod, just a little.

The stadium falls into that magical hush that only happens in the split second before the first pitch of a game—the kind that matters. Sixty feet and six inches separate me from making a statement.

I wind up, driving off the rubber with controlled power. My arm whips forward, the ball exploding from my fingertips at 95 mph, slicing through the air toward the inside corner of the plate. Jared's eyes widen very slightly. He wasn't expecting this much velocity, this much control, but he manages to swing.

Too late.

"Strike one!" the umpire bellows.

The crowd erupts, and I feel a rush of adrenaline surge through my veins. I catch a glimpse of Amy's face. She's beaming like the girlfriend of a fastball king whom she happens to love. This is what we worked for, the two of us together, the perfect matchup.

Jared steps out of the box, adjusting his batting gloves with a scowl. I can read his thoughts like they're written across his forehead: This isn't the same pitcher he faced six months ago.

The catcher calls for a slider. I shake him off. Not yet. I want to establish dominance with the fastball first. He nods, flashing the sign for another heater, this time outside. I wind up and stare down Jared. It's not about intimidation. It's about focus. I know exactly what I want to do with this pitch.

I go into my windup. My mechanics are flawless—the product of countless hours with Amy refining my delivery. This time, I push the fastball to 97 mph, painting the outside corner.

Jared swings and connects, but it's a weak ground ball to short. Our shortstop fields it cleanly and fires to first.

"Out!" the umpire calls.

One down. Twenty-six more to go.

I allow myself a quick glance toward Amy. She gives me a subtle nod—professional, composed, but I can read the love in her eyes. We both know what this means. My first batter I've faced in the World Series, and I've already retired the league's most notorious hitter. I've already proven all those commentators wrong.

Another guy strides up to the plate—a power hitter who swings for the fences. I work him inside, outside, changing speeds and locations. Three pitches later, he's shuffling back to his team's dugout, shaking his head after watching my slider freeze him for strike three.

Two down.

The third batter manages to make contact, but it's a lazy fly ball to center field. Our centerfielder settles under it easily, squeezing his glove around the ball for the final out.

Three up, three down. A perfect first inning.

The crowd roars as I walk off the mound, and my teammates pat me on the back as I reach the dugout. But I don't let myself get caught up in the moment. This is just the first inning of the first game. We have a long ways to go yet.

And I'm ready for it all.

Chapter Twenty-One
All for One

Another day, another chance to show Jared Morris that he's not the sultan of baseball. But this evening, things haven't been going great for me. The Altitude switched to their pinch hitter, and he's damn good. We're on Game Five tonight, so I've got at least two more chances to beat Morris into the ground. Can't say which team is doing the best because, so far, it's been a toss-up.

Come on, man, don't let the Altitude guys wreck your game. Gotta focus on the ultimate goal—winning the World Series.

I grip the bat tighter, watching the pitcher's eyes narrow as he winds up. The fastball comes screaming toward me at ninety-five miles per hour. Time slows. I watch the seams rotating, calculate the trajectory, and—

Swing and a miss. Strike three.

"Dammit," I mutter, trudging back to the dugout where twenty-four pairs of eyes avoid looking at me directly. Another strikeout. My fourth this week.

Amy stands at the edge of the dugout, arms crossed over her Jacksonville Admirals polo. Her expression is unreadable, but I feel the weight of her disappointment dragging me down. Not that I'm blaming her. But I need to get worries about whether I'll screw up out of my head.

"Braddock," she says casually as I pass by her. Just my name. Nothing else needed.

I slump onto the bench, tossing my batting helmet aside. Maybe I'm subconsciously worried I've lost my touch. But no, that isn't the problem. It's Amy. Every time my gaze wanders to her, I lose my focus. Every time I step up to the plate, I'm not just thinking about hitting the ball. I'm thinking about impressing her. Proving I'm still worth the contract. After all, I still have the threat of being traded hanging over me.

"Hey, Charlie, you gonna sit there all day looking like some-one stole your puppy?" Martinez slides in next to me, bumping my shoulder. "It's one at-bat."

"One of many lately," I grumble, grabbing a water bottle and taking a long drink.

From across the field, I spot Jared Morris grinning at me from the Altitude dugout. Even from this distance, I can read the smugness in his posture. He mouths something that looks suspiciously like "washed up."

That dirtbag.

"Don't let him get in your head," Amy advises, coming up behind me. I hadn't noticed she'd moved. Her voice is hushed, meant only for my ears. "That's exactly what he wants."

I grip the water bottle so hard the plastic crackles. "I'm well aware of his tactics."

"Then stop playing into them." Her attention shifts to Morris before returning to me. There's something in her gaze I can't quite read. "You're better than this, Charlie."

Before I can respond, Coach Bennett calls the team together for a quick huddle. He's the head coach, and everyone listens to him. We're down by two in the seventh inning. Not impossible to overcome, but we need to do better.

"All right, listen up," Bennett tells us, his weathered face creased with concentration. "Martinez, you're up next. Braddock, you're on deck after Reynolds."

I need to get my head straight before I'm up again. So in my mind, I prepare to recite the mantra Amy had taught me. But I don't get the chance.

Amy walks by me, her hand briefly touching my shoulder. "Wake up, Charlie. Gotta stay focused."

"What? I am awake—and very focused."

But she's already gone. I caught only a glimpse of her face as I watched her ambling away. Amy and I, we both have jobs to do. She's my coach, and so much more—but on the field, we're strictly business. I love her, and she loves me. That's all the encouragement I need.

Martinez settles into his position at the plate, and I focus on his stance. He connects with the first pitch, sending it soaring into left field. The crowd erupts as he makes it safely to first base.

"That's how it's done!" someone shouts from our dugout.

Reynolds is up next, and I grab my batting helmet, ready to be on deck. I take a few practice swings, feeling the familiar weight of the bat in my hands. The rhythm helps clear my head, pushing out thoughts of Morris and whatever jackass move he might make.

Then Reynolds connects on the third pitch—a solid hit that advances Martinez to second. The crowd's energy surges, and I feel it flow into me as I step toward the plate.

"Braddock's up!" someone shouts from the stands. A mix of cheers and nervous murmurs follows.

I take my position at the plate, digging my cleats into the dirt. The pitcher eyes me warily, and I stare back, refusing to blink first. In my peripheral vision, I see Morris shifting in the outfield, probably hoping I'll send one his way so he can make a play.

Not today, you rat snake.

I block out everything except the pitcher and the ball.

Focus. Breathe. This is what I've trained for my entire life.

The first pitch comes in high—ball one.

But the second pitch catches the outside corner—strike one.

I adjust my grip, rolling my wrists slightly. The crowd noise fades to a distant hum as I lock eyes with the pitcher. He winds up and releases a curveball that starts high then breaks sharply downward.

I see it coming. Time slows again, but this time I'm ready. I swing with everything I've got, feeling the sweet spot of the bat connect with the ball. The crack echoes through the stadium like a gunshot.

The ball rockets toward right-center field, sailing over Morris's outstretched glove. He stumbles backward, cursing loudly enough for me to hear it as I round first base. Martinez scores easily. Reynolds is sprinting toward home, and I'm pushing for a double. The crowd jumps to their feet with a thunderous roar.

I slide into second base just as the throw comes in, kicking up a cloud of dust.

"Safe!" the umpire signals, and our dugout erupts.

I scramble to my feet, brushing the dirt from my uniform, and can't resist glancing toward Morris. His face is twisted with frustration, and he deliberately turns away when our eyes meet. The satisfaction that floods through me is sweeter than any home run.

"That's what I'm talking about, Braddock!" Coach Bennett yells from the dugout, clapping his hands.

But it's Amy's reaction I'm searching for. She stands at the periphery of the dugout wearing a smug smile. She gives me a sly nod, and I swear I can read her thoughts: You've still got it. You always did.

As another batter steps up to the plate, I take my lead off second base, ready to run. My heart is still pounding, not just from exertion but from that look Amy gave me. She's earned that look. My coach worked harder than anyone in the MLB last summer, when I was recovering from my shoulder injury. She refused to let me lie down and give up. Her tactics pissed me off at first, but I quickly realized she knew exactly what she was doing.

"You can't baby an injury like this," she'd informed me back then, her hands firm on my shoulder as she guided me through exercises that made me sweat and curse. "You have to challenge it, or you'll never get back to where you were."

But now, my thoughts return to the present.

The pitcher winds up, and I edge further from second base. The ball connects with the bat, sending a grounder toward third. I take off, rounding third base as the third baseman fumbles the ball. The coach is waving me home frantically, and I dig deep, pumping my legs harder than I have all season.

The throw comes in from the outfield, a bullet aimed straight for home plate. I can see the catcher positioning himself, glove ready. It's going to be close.

I don't slow down. Instead, I lower my shoulder and launch myself into a headfirst slide, my fingers stretching for the plate. The catcher lunges, ball in glove, and I feel the tag brush against my jersey as my hand slaps against home. For a moment, everything goes silent as the umpire hovers over us.

"Safe!" he bellows, thrusting his arms out wide.

The stadium erupts. My teammates pour out of the dugout, and suddenly I'm surrounded and being pounded on the back and shoulders. We're up by one. The momentum has swung our way.

As I untangle myself from the celebratory dogpile, my eyes find Amy again. She's hanging back, maintaining her professional distance, but her smile says everything. I've never wanted to kiss someone more than I want to kiss her right now, but there are about ten thousand witnesses and a strict no-fraternization policy that would get us both fired.

We ignored that policy on the night when we fucked each other like mad in the dugout. After hours, but still…Maybe it was wrong. It felt so damn good, though. Amy promised me the best sex in the history of the universe—her words—if I won us the World Series.

I trot back to the dugout, and she hands me a towel without a word. Our fingers brush, and that familiar spark ignites between us.

"Nice running," she says, her voice neutral but her eyes gleaming with humor.

"Nice coaching…coach," I reply, keeping my tone equally neutral.

Sarcastically so.

The game continues, and we manage to hold onto our lead through the eighth inning. When we take the field for the top of the ninth, the energy in the stadium is electric. The fans are on their feet, stomping and clapping in rhythm. Three outs. That's all we need to take Game Five and push ahead in the series.

I jog out to my position, feeling lighter than I have in weeks. My hit and run might have breathed new life into me and into the team. Morris glares at me from across the field, and I can't help but grin back. Nothing pisses him off more than seeing me succeed.

The first Altitude batter steps up. He's their leadoff man, known for his patience at the plate. Our pitcher, Rodriguez, goes through his familiar routine—adjusting his cap, touching the rosin bag, gazing up at the sky briefly. The first pitch is a strike, painting the outside corner. The second is fouled off.

The count is 0-2.

Now it's time to go for it all the way.

Chapter Twenty-Two
Fastball Revenge

lucked out this time with an 0-2 count—no balls, two strikes. That gives me an advantage, for the moment, and I won't let that opportunity pass me by. Not with Jared Morris at the plate. He's been the thorn in my side for years, the bane of my existence, the insufferable jerk who's been riling me up since our college days.

I adjust my grip on the ball, feeling the familiar seams against my fingertips. The stadium lights catch the sweat beading on my brow as I stare him down from the mound. Jared's signature cocky smirk is firmly in place, and his bat is twitching slightly as he waits for my pitch.

"Come on, Braddock," Jared taunts, half whispering. "Show me what you've got. Or are you still throwing those marshmallows you call fastballs?"

I clench my jaw, refusing to take the bait. Amy has often warned me about letting Morris get under my skin. That's his specialty—not just hitting home runs but hitting nerves.

The catcher pops his mitt open and shut, waiting for me to throw. The noise from the stands fades to a distant hum as I focus on my task. This moment, right here, is everything I'd been fighting for during long months of rehab.

I wind up, muscle memory taking over as the ball flies out of my hand in a blur, cutting through the air with a kind of precision I haven't experienced in ages. For a split second, I see doubt flash across Jared's face.

Perfect. Let the jerk worry.

He swings—too late.

The satisfying smack of leather echoes as the ball hits the catcher's mitt. The umpire's arm shoots up.

"Strike three! You're out!"

The crowd erupts, and I allow myself a small fist pump. Nothing excessive, nothing that would give Jared the satisfaction of knowing how much this matters to me.

"Lucky pitch," Jared snarls, glowering at me as we pass each other.

I don't dignify that with a response and let my pitching speak for itself. Three up, three down—a perfect inning to end the fifth. I'm feeling good tonight. Better than good, actually.

Coach Martinez slaps my back as I descend the dugout steps. "Superb, Braddock. You're dialed in."

"Thanks, Coach." I snag my water bottle and collapse onto the bench, stretching my shoulder. No pain. Just the good kind of fatigue that comes from working hard.

"Keep this up and we might just have ourselves a comeback story," he says with a wink before turning to address the batters who'll be up next inning.

I take another swig of water, observing as our offense takes the field. From the corner of my eye, I catch a glimpse of a familiar figure leaning against the railing near the entrance to the locker rooms. It's Alicia.

What is my ex-wife doing here? Sure, we're friends these days. But Alicia knows I'm with Amy now.

The woman I adore walks into the dugout, sitting down beside me, and I forget all about my ex-wife. Amy rubs her cheek against my shoulder. "You're amazing today, Charlie. I can almost taste victory coming our way. And that's all because of you."

"It's a team sport. I'm one spoke in the wheel, that's all."

She leans closer to whisper, "After the game, let's go back to your place. I bought the massage oil we saw in that little shop..."

"Mm-hm." That's all I can say, since two of my teammates just sat down beside me.

Amy wanders back to the bullpen. I enjoy the view of her sexy ass while she walks away.

"Eyes on the game, Braddock," I mutter to myself, forcing my attention back to the field where Rodriguez has just connected with a fastball, sending it deep into left field. The crowd roars as he rounds first base, and I'm on my feet with the rest of the dugout, pumping my fist in the air.

"That's it, Rod! Keep going!" I shout as he slides safely into second. The momentum is building, electrifying our team. This is what we've been working for all season.

Coach Martinez signals from his position, and Rodriguez nods, understanding the play. Our next batter, Sanchez, saunters up to the plate.

I roll my shoulder, feeling the pleasant burn of muscles that have worked hard but aren't giving out. Not anymore. My gaze drifts back to where I spotted Alicia, but she's gone now. Probably for the best. I need to stay focused, especially with Amy keeping a close eye on me. She gives me a thumbs-up sign, smiling sweetly.

Then she mouths, "Take it all the way!"

Knowing Amy is there, following every moment, makes me feel a hundred feet tall.

"Hey, Braddock," Johnson, our shortstop, nudges me. "Your ex is here with some guy. Thought you should know."

"Uh-huh." As if it matters to me who my ex-wife hangs out with.

I keep track of the plays as best as I can. But my gaze perpetually returns to Amy—her profile lit up by the stadium lights, a slight smile on her lips. She's beautiful, so damn beautiful.

Two more runs in the sixth inning put us up 5-1. When I take the mound again in the seventh, I'm riding high on adrenaline and confidence. The first batter goes down swinging.

The second batter hits a weak grounder to first—an easy out. Then Jared Morris waltzes up to the plate again, and the voltage on the field just got dialed up to a dangerous level.

"Ready for another strikeout, Morris?" I shout, because I just can't help myself. The words poured out before I could stop them.

Jared's gaze narrows. "In your dreams, Chucky."

Amy catches my eye again, grinning and fist-pumping. Just seeing her again gives me the biggest boost ever. Not only a hundred feet tall, but a thousand feet for sure.

I shake off the first signal from my catcher, then the second. I want my fastball for this—the pitch that's working like magic tonight. When I get the sign I want, I nod, wind up, and release.

The ball rockets toward home plate, but even as it leaves my fingertips, I know something's off. It hangs just a fraction too high, and Jared's eyes light up like it's Christmas morning. The crack of bat meeting ball echoes through the stadium, and the high I've enjoyed starts to dwindle. Time slows as I watch the ball sail toward center field, climbing higher and farther. Our center fielder backpedals, then stops and watches helplessly as the ball clears the fence.

Jared takes his time rounding the bases, arms raised in triumph. He makes sure to throw a cocky grin my way as he crosses home plate, pointing directly at me before high-fiving his teammates.

"That's how it's done, Little Chucky!" he calls out, his voice carrying across the field.

I grip the baseball tighter in my hand, fighting the urge to hurl it at his stupid grinning face. Amy jogs up beside me, her hand extended for the ball. "Shake it off, Charlie. One run doesn't lose us the game. Just take a few slow, deep breaths, and then shake it off. Remember the mantra."

"I had him, Coach. I just—"

"I know. Your fastball was working perfectly—until it wasn't."

I inhale deeply, following her guidance despite the frustration boiling in my gut. And I recite the mantra—forget the world, forget the pressure, stay calm and balanced and the game is yours to win.

"Just do that thing we've been practicing. Find your center, and refocus," Amy reminds me. She hands me a new ball with a reassuring nod. "You've got this, Charlie. I'd kiss you for good luck, but that might give Morris a chance to harass you again."

"I won't let him get to me ever again."

She moves closer as if to kiss me but stops halfway there. Instead of giving me a smooch, Amy speaks in a fierce tone. "Now, you go get that rat bastard Jared Morris and grind his face into the dirt."

"You're so hot when you go demonic on Morris." I drop my voice to an even softer whisper. "We'll definitely use that massage oil later."

Amy smirks over her shoulder at me as she jogs back to the bullpen.

I roll my shoulders and find my stance. A new batter is waiting and ready. I erase thoughts of Jared's home run from my mind. One bad pitch doesn't upset me. Not anymore.

The next batter goes down swinging on four pitches. Even with Morris's homer, we're still up 5-2. Not bad at all. I head back to the dugout with my head held high, teammates patting my back as I descend the steps.

"Don't sweat it, Charlie," Phil advises, offering me a cup of water. "We're still up by three."

"I know." I gulp down a long drink. "Thanks, Phil."

Amy jogs into the dugout—to check on me again, I'm sure. Amy Keller might be a tough coach, but she worries about me a little too much. Still, I love that she fusses over me. It's a sign of true love or something like that.

Okay, I secretly love it. And I need to marry that woman as soon as possible. She's my North Star, keeping me aimed in the right direction.

Coach Martinez eyes me from the other side of the dugout. "How's the shoulder feeling, Braddock?"

"Good." And I'm not bullshitting. It's true. No twinges, no shooting pain, just the normal fatigue. "I can go another inning, Coach."

"He's right," Amy concurs. "Charlie's in better shape now than he was before the injury."

Martinez nods, apparently satisfied. "We'll see about another inning. Depends on how our offense does."

Once I'm back on the field, for the eighth inning, I scan the crowd again. There's Alicia, back with the same guy—some tall dude in an expensive-looking suit. They're sitting a few rows behind our dugout. She waves to get my attention. I give her a slight wave too but keep my focus on the game.

The scoreboard shows we've added another run. Six to two—a comfortable lead, but baseball has a way of turning on a dime. I've seen too many late-inning collapses to get overconfident.

"Braddock, you're up for the eighth," Martinez confirms. "Keep it tight, son."

"Will do, Coach." I stand and start my warm-up throws, feeling the pleasant stretch in my shoulder muscles.

Amy approaches with her clipboard, professional as always when others are watching. "Your release point was a little high on that pitch to Morris. Keep your elbow tucked just a hair more."

"Got it." I make the adjustment with my next practice throw. "Better?"

"Perfect." The corner of her mouth twitches into her patented half-smile. "Now go show them what Charlie Braddock is really made of."

I take the mound for the ninth inning with renewed determination. The first batter steps up to the plate, and I struggle to restrain my self-satisfied smile. It's Jared Morris. This is no time to get ahead of myself, though. But as I catch a glimpse of Amy in the bullpen, I feel taller and stronger—only for a second or two. I can sense I'm about to vanquish my enemy at last.

With my fastball.

I adjust my grip on the ball, staring down Jared Morris with a focus so intense everything else blurs around the edges. The roar of the crowd fades to white noise as I wind up. This pitch matters. This moment matters.

The ball leaves my hand like a rocket, blazing toward home plate with the kind of heat I haven't thrown since before my injury. Morris's eyes widen a fraction. He wasn't expecting this kind of velocity from me. Not anymore.

He swings hard but connects with nothing but air.

Strike one.

The crowd goes wild, and I allow myself the briefest smile before refocusing. One good pitch doesn't win the battle. I need two more.

"Lucky pitch," Morris calls out, tapping his cleats with his bat. His petulant expression tells me everything I need to know.

I ignore him, rolling the new ball between my fingers. The catcher flashes the signal—slider, low and outside. I nod, wind up, and deliver. The ball breaks sharply at the last moment, and Morris lunges for it, off balance.

Strike two.

"Still got your number, Morris."

His expression darkens, and his knuckles whiten around the bat handle. "Throw your best, Braddock. I'm waiting."

I prepare myself for the hottest pitch of my life, knowing deep inside that I will wipe out anything Morris has ever done. My fastest pitch ever will destroy my nemesis.

I can feel Amy's eyes on me, her tension mirroring my own. I center myself the way she taught me, repeating my mantra in my head. The catcher signals for the fastball again. My bread and butter. I nod, set my stance, and channel every ounce of strength and technique I've rebuilt over months of grueling rehab. The ball explodes from my hand, a white-hot streak blazing through the humid night air.

Morris swings with everything he's got—and misses by a mile. The satisfying smack of leather as the ball hits the catcher's mitt is the sweetest sound I've ever heard.

"Strike three! You're out!"

But how fast was that pitch? A radar gun will decide. All I can do is wait for the verdict. What do I know for sure? I got my fastball revenge against Jared Effing Morris.

Chapter Twenty-Three
The After Party

The stadium blows up in a deafening roar of screams and applause. I can't help myself—I pump my fist in the air as adrenaline burns through my veins. My teammates rush the mound, surrounding me in a tangle of arms and shouts and pure, unfiltered joy. My heart is racing, and now I really do feel breathless. A pile of players has overtaken me, but I couldn't be happier to get crushed.

"You showed that bastard!" Phil yells, clapping me on the back so hard I nearly stumble.

Through the crush of bodies, I catch sight of Morris slouching back to his dugout, shoulders hunched in defeat. Briefly, our gazes connect, and I detect something beyond his usual arrogance. Maybe it's respect, or possibly shock. Either way, I'll take it. He shakes his head slightly before disappearing into the shadows of the dugout.

"Braddock! Braddock!" The crowd chants my name like I'm some kind of hero. Maybe today, I am.

The celebration continues as we make our way back to our own dugout. Hands slap my back, and voices congratulate me from all directions. The sweet taste of victory is on my tongue, and it's juicier than any beer could ever be.

"Didn't I tell you?" Phil says, his voice rough with emotion. "Didn't I say you had his number?"

I grin, still riding this high. "Yeah, you did. I'll never doubt you again, Phil."

"That curveball in the ninth…" He gestures wildly with his hands. "Pure artistry!"

An announcer comes on over the PA system. "Let's hear it for our hometown hero, Charlie Braddock! His fastball clocked in at…"

Everything seems to freeze while the damn announcer draws it out for as long as possible. I hate dramatic effect. Just fucking tell me. When Amy rushes up to me, wrapping her arms around my waist, we both wait in hushed anticipation. The entire stadium seems to hold its breath.

"One hundred point six!" the announcer virtually screams. "Charlie Braddock is in second place worldwide! Only Nolan Ryan could best that fastball!"

The stadium explodes again, the sound so intense I feel it vibrating through my bones. One hundred point six. Holy shit. I've never thrown that fast in my life. Not in college, not in the minors, not even before my injury.

"Charlie!" Amy races up to me, her eyes wide with excitement. Her hands are still gripping my waist, and I realize I'm holding her too, both of us locked in a moment of unbridled exultation. "Do you have any idea what this means?"

I can barely hear her over the roar of the crowd, but I can read the joy on her face. My teammates are losing their minds around us, jumping and shouting like little kids.

"It means I'm back," I exclaim, my voice cracking with emotion.

Her smile widens. "Damn right you are."

For a fleeting moment, I see something else in her eyes, something that goes beyond professional pride. It's gone before I can be sure, but it leaves me with a strange flutter in my chest that has nothing to do with baseball.

The post-game interviews are a blur. I'm shuttled from one reporter to another, microphones thrust in my face, cameras flashing. I answer on autopilot, spouting the usual clichés about teamwork and perseverance, but inside I'm still reeling. One hundred point six. The number echoes in my head like a mantra.

"How does it feel to silence your critics?" a reporter asks, her pen poised over her notepad.

I pause, considering how to answer. "It feels like…finding something you thought was lost forever."

Later, in the locker room, the celebration continues. Someone's broken out the champagne—against regulations, but no one seems to care tonight. The cork pops with a satisfying thunk, and the bubbly liquid splashes everywhere, drenching jerseys and cleats. The guys are singing some off-key victory anthem they made up on the spot. It's terrible and perfect all at once.

I take a swig directly from the bottle when it's passed to me, the bubbles burning my throat in the best possible way. After a shower and a change of clothes, I head for the exit, still riding the high.

The hallway outside the locker room is quieter, the sounds of celebration muffled behind me. I'm almost to the exit when I see her—Amy leaning against the wall, scrolling through her phone. She's changed out of her coaching gear into jeans and a simple blue top that makes her eyes look even more beautiful, if that's possible.

"There he is," she says. "The man of the hour."

She gazes up at me with what I swear is…adoration.

"Just doing my job, Coach," I say, but I can't keep the grin off my face.

"False modesty doesn't suit you, Braddock." She pushes off the wall and walks toward me. "One hundred point six. That's not just doing your job. That's making history."

The hallway feels smaller suddenly, the air between us charged with something I can't quite name. My heart rate picks up again, and I wonder if she can hear it.

"I couldn't have done it without you," I admit. And it's true. Her relentless pushing, her refusal to let me wallow in self-pity after my injury—she deserves as much credit as I do.

"Don't be so modest." She grasps a handful of my shirt, dragging me closer. "What you did out there on the diamond made me so hot for you. Remember what I suggested earlier, before the all the melee?"

"Hmm, I think I've forgotten." But of course, I haven't.

She catches her lip between her teeth, letting it slide out gradually. "To-night, you'll get the steamiest, raunchiest, most mind-blowing sex of your life, Braddock."

I lean closer until our lips brush. "Are you trying to seduce me, Coach Keller?"

Her laugh is low and sultry. "Is it working?"

"You know damn well it is." My voice sounds rough even to my own ears.

We're standing too close for a coach and player in a public hallway, but right now, I couldn't care less. The victory, the adrenaline, the way she's looking at me—it's all combining into something explosive.

"Your place or mine?" I ask, my hand finding her waist.

Amy's chest rises and falls heavily. "Mine. It's closer."

The drive to her apartment is torture. She insists on taking separate cars—for "appearances," she claims—but the anticipation building between us makes every red light feel like an eternity. I follow her sedan through the Jacksonville streets, the city lights blurring as my mind races ahead to what's waiting for me.

When we finally arrive, I barely remember to lock my car. Amy's already at her door, keys jingling in her hand. The second we're inside, the pretense drops. She tosses her purse onto the floor, and I kick the door shut behind us.

"Get over here," I growl, pulling her against me.

Our lips crash together, hungry and desperate. She tastes like mint and victory. Her hands are everywhere—in my hair, under my shirt, clawing at my back. I press her against the wall, lifting her so her legs wrap around my waist.

"Bedroom," she gasps between kisses. "Down the hall."

I carry her there, our mouths still fused as we hungrily devour each other. It's a miracle we don't crash into anything. Her apartment is neat and minimalist, just like I'd expect from someone as focused as Amy. But I don't have time to appreciate the decor because she's tugging my shirt over my head and running her hands over my chest, tracing the muscles there with an appreciative hum.

"God, Charlie," she breathes. "Do you have any idea how hard it's been not to have you inside me for so long? I know you needed to stay focused on your game, but still…"

"It's been torture for me too, baby." I lower her onto the bed, following her down, my weight pressing her into the mattress. Then I trail wet kisses down her throat, so hungry for this woman that my pulse is pounding in my ears.

"Know what turns me on the most?" she asks while arching beneath me. "Your form. The way your body moves when you pitch. It's like art and sex combined." Her fingers dig into my shoulders. "And then you hit that one-hundred point six, and I nearly lost it right there in the dugout. I wanted to drag you to the ground and ride you like a wild cowgirl."

I laugh against her skin, my hand sliding under her shirt. "So it was my fastball that did it for you, huh?"

"Among other things." She pushes me back just enough to pull her shirt off over her head, revealing a lacy black bra that makes my dick twitch. "I've been planning this for weeks, imagining what I want to do to you—and with you."

"Go on, then. Fuck me, Coach." I drag a finger along the edge of her bra, watching goosebumps rise on her skin as her nipples tighten into stiff little peaks. "Tell me what else you've been planning."

She licks her lips, her gaze glossy, and drags her tongue over her lips again, more slowly this time. "Take off your pants and I'll show you."

The huskiness in her voice is so damn hot.

We're both frantic now, shedding clothes with no regard for where they land. When she's down to just her underwear, I pause to admire her body—the smooth curves, the toned muscles from years of athletic training, the flush spreading across her chest.

"You're staring," she whispers, but I can tell she likes it.

"Can you blame me?" I run my hands up her sides, feeling her shiver. "You're fucking gorgeous, Amy."

She hooks a leg around mine and flips us over with surprising strength, straddling me with a triumphant grin. "My turn to stare."

The woman will give me a heart attack. But who cares?

Her gaze travels down my body so slowly that I feel like I'm burning up from the inside out. Next, she splays her hands over my chest and my abs, tracing every muscle with deliberate slowness. "You know how long I've wanted this? How many nights I've lain awake thinking about having you like this, at my mercy?"

I grip her hips, guiding her against me. "Show me."

Chapter Twenty-Four

A Little Downtime

Amy leans over me, her hair falling around us like a waterfall, and captures my mouth in a kiss that's all tongue and teeth and scorching need. I reach behind her to unhook her bra, and she sits up to let it fall away. Her breasts are perfect—full and firm with dusky nipples that beg for my attention. I coast my hands over her creamy skin before cupping those gorgeous mounds. Amy gasps when my thumbs brush across her nipples, her eyes fluttering shut briefly before zeroing in on mine with an intensity that steals my breath.

"Charlie," she whispers, grinding down against me, the friction maddening even through our remaining clothes.

I lean toward her to draw one perfect peak into my mouth, circling my tongue around it before sucking gently. She tangles her fingers in my hair, clinging to me while a carnal moan spills from her lips. God, I need to consume her, from those tits to her folds and everywhere in between. The sound drives me out of my mind. I switch to her other breast, giving it the same treatment while my hands glide down to grasp her hips.

The scent of her lust suffuses the air, and I shimmy lower until her mound is millimeters from my face. Then I spread those lips tenderly, sinking into them, relishing the slickness, the delicious flavor of her essence. Amy's juices cover my face, musky and sweet and intoxicating. I lap at her hungrily, exploring every fold and crevice of her most intimate region with my tongue. She rocks against my mouth, her thighs trembling.

"Oh, shit, Charlie," she pants, her voice breaking on my name. "Right there. Don't stop."

I have no intention of stopping. I circle her clit with my tongue before gently tugging it between my lips. Her hips jerk forward. I grasp her buttocks to hold her steady against my mouth. I work one finger inside her, then two, curling them to find the spot that makes her cry out. Amy's breathing grows ragged, her movements more desperate.

I glance up at the length of her body spread out before me and find her watching me. Her lips are parted, her chest is flushed. The sight of her—strong, commanding Amy Keller—coming undone above me is the most erotic thing I've ever seen. I redouble my efforts, wanting—needing—to make her crumble in my hands.

"Charlie, I'm—" she gasps, and then she's coming. Her inner walls clench around my fingers as her thighs tighten around my head. I don't let up, drawing out her pleasure until she's shaking and pulling away, suddenly too sensitive.

Amy collapses beside me, her chest heaving. A fine sheen of sweat seems to make her skin glow in the dim light. I can't help but gape at her—this woman who's been driving me nuts both on and off the field.

"Your turn," she declares after catching her breath.

Before I can respond, she's straddling me again, her nimble fingers making quick work of my belt and zipper.

I hoist my hips to help her slide my jeans and boxers down and off my legs. I'm so hard it's almost painful. When Amy wraps her graceful hand around my length, I hiss through my teeth.

"Jesus, Amy," I groan as she strokes me slowly, her grip firm but gentle.

Her eyes meet mine, twinkling with humor and lust. "You like that?"

"Oh, you know I do."

As she bows her head, ever lower, the first touch of her tongue against my flesh nearly shatters my self-control. But Amy takes her time, exploring me with the same thoroughness I showed her, and I finally understand why she went wild in my arms. This woman might do the same thing to me—and I will love it. My hands fist in the sheets as she takes me into her mouth, the silken heat of it making me buck my hips involuntarily.

"Sorry," I mutter, trying to control myself.

Amy pulls back just enough to speak. "Don't apologize. I want you thrashing and incoherent."

She flashes a wicked grin just before she takes me deep again, her hand working at what her mouth can't reach. I thread my fingers through her hair, not guiding, just needing to touch her. The sight of Amy Keller—my tough coach—with her lips wrapped around me is almost too much to bear. My body tenses while pressure builds at the base of my spine.

"Amy," I warn, tugging gently at her hair. "I'm so close."

She releases me, crawling up my body until we're face to face again. "I want you inside me, filling me up, making me come again. But this time, we'll explode together."

"Do you have…?"

She reaches for her discarded jeans, fishing a foil packet from the pocket. "Always prepared."

When she smirks in the sexiest way, it does things to me I can't describe. Hot things. Filthy things.

I snatch the condom from her, but she brushes my hand away.

"You want me to do this, I can tell," she whispers, her tone husky, and she rips that packet open with her teeth.

And damn if my breath doesn't catch as she rolls the latex down my length, her touch both tender and teasing. Then she's positioning herself above me, her eyes locked on mine as she gradually sinks down. We both moan as I fill her completely, her inner walls stretching to accommodate me.

"Fuck," I breathe, my hands flying to her hips.

Amy remains motionless for a moment, adjusting to the feel of me inside her. Then she begins to move, setting a rhythm that has my toes curling. She's magnificent above me—strong, confident, taking what she wants. Her breasts bounce with every movement, and I reach up to cup them, pinching her nipples lightly between my fingers.

"You feel so good," she gasps, leaning into my touch. "Been thinking about this since I first saw you on that mound."

The admission sends heat surging through my veins. I thrust up to meet her movements, our bodies finding a perfect rhythm together. It's like we've been doing this dance forever, anticipating each other's moves, responding to every subtle cue.

"Same," I growl in between ragged breaths. "Wanted you from day one."

The woman I love smiles down at me, a genuine smile that transforms her face and somehow makes her even more beautiful. I pull her down for a kiss, messy and desperate, all tongue and hot breath as we continue to move together. When I subtly change the angle, she cries out against my mouth.

"There," she pants. "Oh, yes, right there."

I grasp her hips firmly, making sure to hit that same spot with every thrust. She squirms and arches her neck, panting and thrashing. I can feel her body tensing up, a sure sign of an impending climax. My own release is building too, the pressure coiling tight.

"I'm almost there," I warn her, my voice raw with need. "So fucking close, Amy."

"Me too," she gasps. "Oh god, Charlie, I can't hold back much longer."

"Then don't, baby."

I shove a hand between us, finding her clit with my thumb. She jerks at the contact, a strangled cry escaping her lips. Her inner walls flutter around me, and that's all it takes to hurl me over the edge. My orgasm crashes through me, intense and all-consuming. I punch into her once, twice, three times more until I blow apart inside her, shouting my pleasure to the heavens. Amy follows a heartbeat later, her body clenching around me as she throws her head back, my name spilling from her lips like a prayer.

For a minute or two, the room holds nothing but our ragged breathing and pounding hearts. Then she collapses on top of me, her sweaty skin pressed against mine, her breaths hot against my neck. I wrap my arms around her, holding her close as we both come down from an incredible high. My heart is still racing, blood pounding in my ears as I stroke her back, feeling the curve of her spine, the softness of her skin.

"Damn, Braddock," she murmurs against my collarbone. "If you played baseball like you fuck, you would've won every World Series in the past thirty years."

I chuckle. "Maybe that's what I've been missing—a good woman who knows how to fuck. Should we add this to my training regimen, Coach?"

Amy lifts her head, and her tousled hair makes her even more appealing. "I'd say it has potential. Definitely improves your stamina."

I sweep a lock of hair from her face, abruptly struck by how beautiful she is in this state. Flushed and disheveled, completely satisfied. Vulnerable in a way I've never seen before. Yes, I want to spend the rest of my life with this woman.

"What's wrong?" she asks. "You look so…blissful."

"It's nothing." As soon as I spoke those words, I realized I needed to correct myself. "Actually, it isn't nothing. You're just…beautiful. So damn beautiful."

A hint of color rises in her cheeks that has nothing to do with our recent exertion. She looks away, and I see the coach I know beginning to resurface—the woman who keeps her walls up, who never lets anyone see her sweat.

I nuzzle her cheek with my nose, and suddenly, I need to blurt out something that I've been thinking about for quite a while. "Amy, would you like to meet my family? We have a couple days off this week."

"Wanna show off your girlfriend, huh?"

"Yeah, maybe." I give her a quick kiss. "I love you, Amy, and I know my family will love you too."

"Sounds great." She hesitates, then bows her head. "Would you, um, mind if I invited my mom to the get-together?"

"Of course I don't mind. Can't wait to meet her." I wiggle my eyebrows. "She might be my mother-in-law pretty soon."

Amy gives my chest a playful push. "Don't get ahead of yourself, Braddock."

Damn, I really do love this woman.

Chapter Twenty-Five
When Families Meet

Two whole days off. It isn't often that I get this kind of opportunity—not simply a brief respite, but also the chance for Amy and me to blend our families. I want to marry that woman. But I should probably wait until after the multi-family gathering before I pop the question.

Right now, I'm all alone in Braddockville. Amy took off to Cooperstown to retrieve her mom. Okay, maybe I'm not totally alone, and maybe the Braddocks don't have our own town. Worrying about the impending collision of families might've made me a tiny bit anxious.

No, that's dumb. I am not anxious. That would be pathetic.

Everyone is gathered in the living room waiting for our guests to arrive.

"Chill out, Charlie," my sister Kaitlyn says, rolling her eyes at me. "Your girl will be here soon."

Lauren chimes in too. "That's right. Sit down and shut up, little brother."

Sydney just shakes her head, staying out of the fracas as usual.

Then the doorbell rings, and I leap out of my chair. I race to the door before anybody can tell me not to do it and swing the door wide open. But it's not Amy standing there. No, it's Alicia—and that guy I'd seen her with a while back.

My ex-wife smiles almost shyly. That's not like her at all.

Alicia grins at me. "Hi Charlie. Surprise!"

I gape at her, my mouth suddenly dry. Alicia's wearing jeans and a flowy white top—casual but still immaculate, just like she always is. Her companion stands slightly behind her, his hand hovering near the small of her back without quite touching it.

"What are you doing here?" I finally ask.

"I heard about the family gathering. Your mom invited me." She tucks a strand of hair behind her ear, a nervous gesture I remember all too well. "This is Teddy, by the way."

Teddy Whoever extends his hand. "Nice to finally meet you, Charlie. Heard a lot about you. I'm Theodore Freeman, but you can call me Teddy."

I shake his hand on autopilot while my brain scrambles to process what's happening. My ex-wife is at my family gathering—the one where I'm supposed to be introducing my girlfriend to everyone.

"Who is that?" my sister Sydney calls out from behind me. Her tone is way too interested for my comfort.

"It's, uh..." I fumble for words, still blocking the doorway.

Alicia peers around me and waves. "Hi Sydney! Hi Lauren! Hi Kaitlyn! Long time no see."

That's all it takes. My sister Kaitlyn practically bulldozes me aside, throwing her arms around my ex-wife like they're sorority sisters at a reunion. "Oh my god, Alicia! Mom didn't tell us you were coming!"

I shoot a desperate look at Sydney, who has appeared in the hallway. She gives me a sympathetic grimace and a tiny shrug. Her meaning is crystal-clear. Everyone knew about this but me.

"Come in, come in," Lauren is saying, practically dragging Alicia inside.

Teddy offers his hands to my youngest sister. "Pleasure to meet you, Kaitlyn. Are all the Braddock women as lovely as you?"

He's laying it on awfully thick. But I guess he's trying to impress...somebody. Can't be me. If he's hitting on my sister, I'll deck him. But he keeps his compliments pretty tame as everyone returns to the living room. I'm still standing half-dazed at the open door when my phone vibrates in my pocket.

It's a text from Amy: *About 15 mins away. Mom is SO excited to meet everyone!*

My stomach drops to somewhere around my ankles. Fifteen minutes. I have fifteen minutes to figure out what the hell is happening and why my ex-wife is currently making herself comfortable in my parents' living room with some guy called Teddy.

"Charlie, honey, close the door. You're letting all the air conditioning out," my mom shouts from somewhere inside the house, probably the kitchen. She must've sneaked out to fix a snack for us.

I step back inside and shut the door, feeling like I'm sealing my own fate. When I return to the living room, Alicia is perched on the sofa, Teddy beside her, while my sisters have formed a semicircle around them as if they're the main attraction at a zoo. I settle onto the sofa and cross my arms to study the new guy more closely.

"So, Teddy," I begin, emphasizing his name. "What do you do for a living."

He whispers something to Alicia, then faces me. "I'm the pinch hitter for the Aspen Altitude."

I think I just did a double take, like a cartoon character. The world tilts slightly, then rights itself. Of all the teams in the league, he had to be with our biggest rivals. I can feel everyone's eyes on me, waiting for my reaction.

"The Altitude," I repeat slowly, keeping my voice neutral. "That's…interesting."

Alicia's eyes widen a smidge. She knows exactly what this revelation means to me. The Admirals and the Altitude have the fiercest rivalry in the league, and here's my ex-wife dating one of them.

"I'm their utility man," Teddy continues smoothly. "But I've been getting more regular starts lately. Coach says I've got a good eye."

"Uh-huh."

"Charlie's with the Admirals," Kaitlyn pipes up helpfully, as if anyone in this room doesn't know that.

"Yeah, I 'm aware," Teddy confirms with a slight smile. "Been following your career since college. You've got quite an arm."

I can't tell if he's being genuine, or if there's a hidden barb in there somewhere. Athletes from rival teams don't exactly exchange friendship bracelets.

"Thanks," I reply stiffly. "Your batting average has been decent this season."

"Decent?" Alicia raises an eyebrow. "He's hitting .320."

Of course she knows his stats. Of course she's defending him. I grind my teeth but then force myself to relax and give him a polite smile. "That's what I said. Decent."

The tension in the room ratchets up a notch.

Sydney clears her throat and jumps up. "Anyone want something to drink? Mom made her famous strawberry lemonade."

"I'd love some," Teddy says, breaking our staring contest.

Sydney disappears to get the drinks, and I'm left staring at my ex-wife and her new boyfriend. The boyfriend who plays for our biggest rivals. The boyfriend who is currently sitting in my parents' living room like he belongs here.

"So, how did you two meet?" Lauren asks, leaning forward, just waiting for some juicy gossip.

Alicia and Teddy exchange a glance, a private communication passing between them that makes my stomach twist.

"Actually, we met at a charity event in Denver," Alicia explains. "I was there representing the magazine I work for, and Teddy was one of the athletes auctioning off a date for charity."

"Did you bid on him?" Kaitlyn asks with a sly grin.

Alicia laughs, the sound so familiar that I have a brief flashback to our marriage. "No, but we ended up talking at the after-party."

Lauren aims her best big-sister stare at me. "Charlie, I know you're not jealous of Teddy. That would be stupid."

Kaitlyn grins. "No, Charlie isn't jealous. He's protective of Alicia, that's all. They were married for a long time."

"That's over now," I interject. "But Alicia is still a good friend, and I'm sure Teddy will be too."

Did those words actually come out of my mouth?

The doorbell rings again, and I nearly trip over my own feet getting to it. This time, it must be Amy.

I yank open the door, and there she is—chestnut hair slightly windblown, green eyes bright with excitement, looking more beautiful than ever in a simple green dress that hangs down just below her knees. Her mother stands beside her—an older version of Amy with the same warm smile but with gray hair instead of brown.

"Charlie!" Amy throws her arms around me, and I hold her tight, breathing in her familiar scent. For a moment, everything is right with the world.

"Hey," I whisper against her hair. "You finally made it."

She pulls back, searching my face. "Is everything okay? You look like you've seen a ghost."

"Not a ghost exactly," I mutter. "More like an ex-wife."

Amy freezes. "What?"

I clear my throat. "Alicia's here. With her new boyfriend. Who, by the way, plays for the Altitude."

The color drains from Amy's face. "The Altitude? As in your team's biggest rivals?"

"That would be the one." I try to keep my voice light. "Our surprise family gathering just got a whole lot more surprising."

Amy's mother steps forward, extending her hand. "I'm Pamela Keller. You must be Charlie. I've heard so much about you."

I shake her hand, grateful for the momentary distraction. "It's great to meet you, Mrs. Keller. Please, come in."

"Call me Pam," she insists with a warm smile that reminds me so much of Amy.

I lead them inside, my hand firmly clasping Amy's. Her fingers are cold, and I give them a reassuring squeeze. I whisper "it's going to be fine," though I'm not entirely sure I believe that myself.

We enter the living room together, and everyone turns to look at us. Alicia's eyes widen slightly when she sees Amy, then she quickly composes herself. Teddy watches the exchange with interest, his arm casually draped across the back of the sofa behind Alicia.

"Everyone," I announce, "this is Amy Keller and her mother, Pam."

My sisters immediately swarm them, offering hugs and introductions. Amy handles the onslaught with grace, laughing at something Kaitlyn says while Pam starts chatting with my mom who's appeared from the kitchen. I stand here like an idiot, watching the two halves of my life collide.

"Hey Charlie," Alicia says, suddenly beside me. I didn't even notice her approach. "This is awkward, huh?"

"No kidding. As long as my sisters don't turn this into a block party, I think we'll all be okay."

A few minutes later, Lauren corners me and Amy in the kitchen where we're hunting for booze. She announces, "Charlie, you picked the right one this time."

Yeah, I finally did.

Chapter Twenty-Six
The Big News

After two days with my family and Amy's mom, I'm more determined than ever to do what I've should've done weeks ago. I need to pop the question. My sisters played a big role in convincing me to go for it, but honestly, I've been ready for this moment since the day I met Amy. However, before I can get down on one knee, my big sister Lauren feels obliged to give me romance advice.

"Charlie, please don't rush this," Lauren says, adjusting my tie for the third time. "You need to make sure the moment is perfect."

I roll my eyes but let her fuss anyway. "I will not mess it up. I've rehearsed what I'm going to say at least fifty times."

"It's not about rehearsing. It's about feeling." She lays her hand over my heart. "What are you feeling right now?"

"Honestly? Like I might throw up." I check my pocket again, making sure the ring is still there. The small velvet box has been burning a hole in my pants for weeks.

Lauren laughs. "That's normal. When Doug proposed to me, he was so nervous he dropped the ring in my champagne glass."

"Yeah, well, I'm planning to keep a tighter grip." I glance at my watch. "Amy's mom should be keeping her busy for another hour, which gives me just enough time to get everything set up at the ballpark."

"I still can't believe you're proposing on a baseball field." My big sister shakes her head, smiling at me fondly.

"It's the place where we fell in love. Where else would I do it?" I check my reflection in the mirror one more time. The fancy suit feels constricting after spending most of my life in baseball uniforms and workout clothes, but Amy deserves the best of everything. I would jump into a volcano to prove my love to her.

Doug appears in the doorway, jingling his car keys. "The florist just called. Everything's set up at the pitcher's mound like you wanted."

My stomach does another flip. "Thanks, man. I appreciate your help with all this."

He claps me on the shoulder. "Are you kidding? I've been waiting for this day since you two finally stopped pretending to hate each other."

I take a deep breath and attempt to calm my nerves. "I just want it to be perfect for her, you know?"

Lauren touches my arm. "Charlie, you could propose to that woman in a parking lot with a lollipop for a ring, and she'd still say yes. Amy loves you."

"I know she does." And it's true. After everything we've been through—my rivalry with Jared, the coaching struggles, even my career-threatening injury—Amy has stood by me, encouraging me to keep outdoing my own stats. "But Lauren, Amy deserves the fairy tale. Every sappy minute of it."

"Then let's get you to your ballpark, Prince Charming." Lauren gives me one final inspection before nodding her approval.

The drive to Jacksonville Admirals Stadium feels both too long and too short. Every stoplight has me checking my phone, making sure Amy hasn't caught on to our plan. Her mom promised to keep her occupied with dress shopping—for Lauren's twelve-year-old daughter. Since Amy adores my niece, it's the perfect ruse.

I can't wait until we have kids of our own.

Doug pulls into the stadium parking lot, turning toward me. "Just speak from the heart, Charlie. That's all any woman wants."

My mouth suddenly feels dry. "Thanks for the pep talk, Doug."

The stadium feels different when it's empty—larger somehow, more imposing. My footsteps echo as I walk across the concrete concourse, past the silent concession stands and team shops. This place has been my second home for years, but today it feels like hallowed ground.

When I step out onto the field, I'm in awe. The grounds crew have outdone themselves. The pitcher's mound is surrounded by a circle of roses—red and white, the Admirals' colors. Tiny lanterns line the base paths, ready to be lit as the sun sets. It's simple but perfect, just as I requested.

"Mr. Braddock, everything looks perfect," the head groundskeeper calls from behind me.

I turn to shake his hand, grateful for his help. "Thanks, Mike. I can't tell you how much this means to me."

"After all you've done for this team? It's the least we could do." He gestures toward the mound. "I'll have the guys light those lanterns about fifteen minutes before sunset. That'll give you the perfect glow when you pop the question."

As Mike walks away, I step onto the pitcher's mound—my domain for so many years. The familiar feel of the clay beneath my dress shoes centers me. This is where I belong. Where we belong.

I pull out my phone and check the time. Fifteen minutes until the woman I love arrives. Doug and Lauren are bringing Amy here under the pretense of picking up some equipment I supposedly left behind. It's a flimsy excuse, but Amy rarely questions anything where I'm concerned, and vice versa. I pace around the mound, rehearsing my speech one more time. The words feel clumsy on my tongue, inadequate for everything I want to tell her. How do you fill so much love, frustration, growth, and passion into a single moment?

My phone buzzes with a text from Lauren: *Operation Fastball is a go. ETA 15 minutes.*

I wipe my sweaty palms on my pants and check my pocket again. The ring is still there, nestled in blue velvet—a princess-cut diamond surrounded by two small sapphires, the exact shade of Admirals blue. The jeweler had called it serendipitous. I call it fate.

Mike reappears with two other groundskeepers, and they move silently around the field, lighting the lanterns one by one. The field gradually glows with a warm, golden light that makes everything feel magical. The clouds have cleared just enough to let the setting sun paint the sky in shades of pink and orange. Even the weather is cooperating with my plan.

I straighten my tie for what must be the hundredth time today. The stadium lights have been turned off, creating an intimate atmosphere in this massive space that usually holds thousands of screaming fans. Tonight, it's exclusively for us.

My phone buzzes yet again.

It's Lauren: *We're walking through the tunnel now. Are you ready?*

I hurriedly type a response: *As ready as I'll ever be.*

The sound of voices echoes from the dugout tunnel, and my heart leaps into my throat. I recognize Amy's laugh immediately, the bright, unguarded sound that charms me every time.

"What about Charlie?" Amy asks. "I know he's forgetful, but this is ridiculous. You didn't even tell me what I'm supposed to be looking for—"

Amy's voice cuts off abruptly as she emerges from the tunnel. Her eyes go wide. She takes in the scene—the lanterns, the roses, me standing alone on the pitcher's mound in a suit that suddenly feels too tight around my collar. For a moment, she doesn't move. The last rays of sunlight glisten on her chestnut hair, creating a halo effect that steals my breath away. Even in jeans and a simple blouse, she's the most beautiful woman I've ever seen.

Then Lauren gives Amy a little shove, encouraging her to jog over to me. When she doesn't move, my sister gives her a firmer push forward.

Lauren and Doug retreat into the tunnel, granting us privacy.

Amy shuffles toward me slowly, seeming both confused and astonished. The lantern light casts a warm glow on her face as she steps onto the pitcher's mound. "Charlie, what is all this?"

I clasp her hands and steady myself. All my rehearsed words evaporate. I'm a pitcher without a game plan, operating purely on instinct. "I wanted to bring you here, where it all began for us."

She glances around at the roses, the lanterns, the empty stadium that somehow feels more alive than during a sold-out game. "This is astonishing and beautiful, Charlie."

"You are beautiful." I squeeze her hands. "Amy, do you remember the first time we met on this field? You told me my fastball was decent, but my attitude needed work." I smile at the memory. "You weren't wrong."

Amy bites her lip while the first shimmer of tears gathers in her eyes. "I was pretty harsh back then. But you needed someone to challenge you."

"I needed you," I correct. "Just didn't know it yet."

The stadium is silent except for our voices and the distant sounds of the city. The intimacy of this massive space, normally filled with thousands of fans, seems out of context yet also perfectly right.

"Charlie Braddock, are you getting sentimental on me?" Amy teases, but her voice wavers.

"I'm about to get a lot more sentimental." Sucking in a big breath, I drop to one knee, right here on the pitcher's mound where I've thrown countless fastballs and where, slightly more than a year ago, Amy first stormed into my life, changing everything.

Her hands fly to her mouth. "Oh my god. Charlie…"

With shaking fingers, I pull the velvet box from my pocket and open it, revealing the ring that's been burning a hole in my pocket for weeks. The sapphires catch the lantern light, and the diamonds twinkle like stars.

"Amy Keller," I begin, my voice surprisingly even. "You walked into my life like a curveball I never saw coming. You challenged me, pushed me, and made me a better player and a better man."

A tear slips down her cheek, and she doesn't bother to wipe it away.

"I've faced down the toughest batters in the league, but nothing has ever made my heart race like you do. Nothing has ever felt as right as loving you." I pause to collect myself, suddenly overwhelmed by this moment. "You are my teammate, my partner, my best friend. And I want to spend every day of my life showing you that this isn't just a good inning—it's the whole damn game." I gaze up at her, my throat tight and overcome with emotion. "Amy Joanne Keller, will you marry me?"

For one terrifying second, she just stares at me, tears streaming freely now. Then she breaks into the most radiant smile I've ever seen.

"Yes," she whispers. Then louder: "Yes, Charles Joshua Braddock! Yes! Of course I'll marry you."

My hands are shaking so badly I almost drop the ring—Lauren would never let me live that down—but I manage to slide it onto Amy's finger. It fits perfectly. I rise and drag her into my arms, lifting her off her feet in a spin that makes her laugh through her joyful tears. When I set her down, she frames my face with her hands. I lean in to press my lips to hers, imbuing the kiss with all the love for this woman that I have inside me. The taste of her tears mingles with our kiss, salty and sweet at the same time.

"I love you," I murmur against her lips. "More than anyone or anything in the whole wide world."

"And I love you just as much." Amy pulls back so she can admire the ring, her eyes wide and glistening. "Charlie, it's perfect. The sapphires—they're Admirals blue."

"Yeah, I noticed." I smile and wink. "What else would I give my fiancée? We're both baseball fanatics."

Suddenly, the stadium lights flash on, and cheers erupt from the tunnel. My family pours onto the field—not just Lauren and Doug, but my parents and grandmother too. Amy's mom is also here. Everyone rushes toward us with open arms and tearful smiles. We're celebrating more than my engagement but also the biggest moment in my professional career.

Chapter Twenty-Seven
The World Series, Part One

Today, I'm in the city of Aspen, Colorado, on the mound at Altitude Park, ready for the first game of the World Series. Naturally, the Assitudes were selected as our opponents. It's the culmination of everything we've fought for all season. The stands are packed with fans from both sides, a sea of Admirals blue clashing with the Altitude's forest green. The thin mountain air feels crisp in my lungs, different from the humid heat of Jacksonville.

I adjust my cap and dig my cleats into the red clay of the mound. The ball feels solid in my hand, the seams rough against my fingertips. I've thrown thousands of pitches in my career, but none as important as the ones I'll throw tonight.

Decker Johnson, the Altitude's star slugger, stands in the batter's box. We have history between us. Last season, he took me deep twice in one game, a memory that still burns. His self-assured smile tells me he remembers too.

"Just like old times, eh, Braddock?" he calls out, tapping his bat against home plate.

Something about his bat seems…different. Johnson taps home plate again. Is that…No, it can't be. But I'd swear he has…

A torpedo bat. I'd recognize the bowling-pin profile of the torpedo bat anywhere. But this is the first time I've encountered one. The

Altitude must be really worried about the Admirals trouncing them if they need to trot out a new weapon. I've heard a lot about torpedo bats, but I'm not sure I want to try it. Feels like cheating somehow.

No time to worry about that. The game has begun.

I narrow my gaze, blocking out the roar of the crowd. All that exists is this moment, this batter, this pitch. Coach Martinez gives me the sign from the dugout—fastball, high and inside. My specialty. I nod discreetly. Then I wind up, channeling all my focus into my grip. The pitch flies from my hand like a bullet, exactly where I want it. Decker swings—and misses.

Strike one.

Cheers erupt from the Admirals fans. First blood has been drawn, but I guess Decker must not have practiced enough with his torpedo bat. He's clever, though, and I'm sure he'll get up to speed quickly.

"Lucky pitch," Decker grumbles, but I can see the doubt creeping into his eyes.

I glance quickly toward our dugout and catch Tripp giving me a thumbs up. It's always good to know your teammates have your back. The catcher signals for another fastball, but I shake him off. Decker's expecting it now. I'll give him a change-up instead, strictly to mess with his timing.

I go into my windup again. The ball leaves my hand looking like heat but arrives fifteen miles per hour slower. Decker lunges forward, his weight shifting too early.

"Strike two!" The umpire's voice booms across the diamond.

Decker steps out of the box, frustration evident in the tight set of his shoulders. He takes a practice swing with that torpedo bat, the wood piercing the air with a distinctive whoosh. The altered barrel clearly gives it different aerodynamics. If he connects solidly, that thing could send the ball into orbit.

Focus, Charlie. Don't let fancy gear trip you up.

The catcher signals for a curveball, low and away. I nod, but my mind races with calculations. Decker's stance has shifted slightly. He's compensating for the bat's different weight distribution. Smart. I need to be smarter.

I wind up and release, watching the ball spin and break. For a heart-stopping moment, I think he's read my pitch. His eyes track the ball with laser focus, and the torpedo bat begins its arc.

But my curve breaks sharply at the last second, just beyond the reach of his swing.

"Strike three! You're out!" The umpire's call is music to my ears.

The Admirals fans erupt in cheers once more. I allow myself a quick fist pump as I catch the return throw from the catcher. Decker stalks back to the dugout, his face like a thunder cloud. One down.

Somebody new approaches the plate, but my mind is still on Decker and that torpedo bat. The way he adjusted so quickly to its weight tells me he's been practicing with it. I squint at the batter, trying to determine what sort of bat he's using. I groan. Damn, he's got a torpedo bat too. This won't be the last I see of it tonight, that much is certain.

I strike out the next batter with three straight pitches, barely registering the mechanics, but I can tell he's getting the hang of his new toy. My body knows what to do even when my mind wanders. The third batter grounds out to short, and just like that, the inning is over.

As I jog back to the dugout, the cool mountain air fills my lungs. The elevation makes everything feel different here—the ball carries farther, breaks differently. Home field advantage for the Altitude in more ways than one.

"Nice work, Braddock," Amy calls out as I descend the steps into the dugout. She smiles, giving my arm a light punch.

"Thanks, Coach." I grab my water bottle and take a long swig. My teammates surround me, offering fist bumps and words of encouragement.

Tripp slides onto the bench beside me. "That torpedo bat's something else, huh?"

"Yeah, it really is. Johnson's already adjusting to it." I wipe sweat from my forehead with my sleeve. "How are we supposed to counter that?"

"Same way we always do. Pitch smart." Tripp's confidence is unwavering, a quality I admire. "Besides, we get a crack at them too. They're available to both teams."

Something about it still doesn't sit right with me. Baseball's always been about the purity of the contest—pitcher versus batter, skill against skill. These new bats feel like they're tilting the scales.

Guess I'm just behind the times.

Our batters head to the on-deck circle as we're up to bat. I watch our leadoff hitter, Marcus, examining one of the torpedo bats with a mixture of curiosity and skepticism.

"You planning to try it?" I ask him.

He hefts the bat, testing its weight. "Might as well. If they're using them, we need to keep up. Right?"

"Guess so." But I can't shake my unease. It isn't solely about keeping up. It's about what these bats mean for the game going forward.

The Altitude's pitcher, Santiago Vega, is a shrewd lefty with a wicked slider. He stares down Marcus as he steps into the box with his torpedo bat. The first pitch is a fastball that Marcus fouls off awkwardly, the bat's unusual weight distribution throwing off his timing.

"It's all in the follow-through!" Tripp calls out.

Marcus adjusts his grip, nodding. His second swing connects better—a sharp line drive that the shortstop barely snags. One out.

I lean forward on the bench, studying Vega's motion, the way the ball leaves his hand. If we're going to beat these guys, I need to pick up every advantage I can.

Our second batter, Rodriguez, steps up with a traditional bat. Bold choice. He works the count full before slapping a single through the gap between short and third. A murmur runs through our dugout. The old ways might still have some merit.

"See that?" I nudge Tripp. "Traditional bat, traditional hit."

"Yeah, but watch this," Tripp says, nodding toward Jameson, our power hitter, who's approaching the plate with a torpedo bat in hand.

Jameson's swing is a thing of beauty—fluid and powerful, connecting with the ball just below its center. The crack reverberates through the stadium as the ball rockets toward the outfield. The torpedo bat's distinctive profile follows through as Jameson watches the ball soar.

For a moment, I think it's gone—a home run in the first inning would set the perfect tone. But the thin mountain air plays tricks. What would be a sure homer in Jacksonville hangs just long enough for the center fielder to make a leaping catch at the wall.

"Damn!" Jameson slams his bat down as he returns to the dugout.

"At home, that would've been gone," I tell him, offering a consolatory pat on the shoulder. But we've locked horns with the Altitude many times, and we never suffered this type of problem.

"Yeah. Altitude Park's a bitch." Jameson examines the torpedo bat with newfound respect. "Got good pop, though."

Our next batter strikes out, ending the inning scoreless. As I walk back toward the mound for the second inning, I can't help but glance at the Altitude's dugout. Their players are huddled together, talking strategy. Decker catches my eye and smirks, tapping his torpedo bat against his cleats.

Game on.

The next few innings pass in a blur of concentration and sweat. The score remains tied at zero, a pitcher's duel between me and Vega. My fastball is working well today, hitting corners with precision. But I'm having to work twice as hard with those torpedo bats in play. Every pitch needs to be perfect.

By the sixth inning, fatigue starts creeping in. The thin mountain air doesn't help, though I'm still unsure of how much the elevation in Aspen could possibly affect us. Every breath seems to deliver less oxygen than I need. But I refuse to show weakness, especially to Decker, who's due up third this inning.

The first batter grounds out to first, an easy play. I strike out the second batter on four pitches. Then Decker swaggers to the plate, that damned torpedo bat resting casually on his shoulder.

"Getting tired, Braddock?" he calls out, his voice carrying across the diamond. "That mountain air's no joke, huh?"

I ignore the taunt, focusing instead on Tripp's signals. Fastball away. I shake my head. Curve? Another shake. Slider. That's the one.

I wind up and deliver, putting everything I have into the pitch. The ball spins toward the plate, breaking sharply at the last moment. But Decker's ready. The torpedo bat connects with a sound that's different from normal wood—deeper, more resonant. The ball rockets toward left field, a line drive that keeps rising.

My heart sinks as I watch it sail over the fence. Home run. The Altitude fans erupt in cheers as Decker rounds the bases with a triumphant fist pump.

1-0, Altitude.

Despite our best efforts, we lose the game. But this is only game one in the series.

Amy sits down beside me in the dugout. "You lost one game, Charlie. It's not the end of the world."

"Yeah, but our next game is here in Aspen too. I'm completely exhausted." I swipe my jersey over my face, mopping up the sweat. "We've played at Altitude Stadium before, but something's different this time."

"Maybe you're anxious about the torpedo bats."

I shrug. Who the hell knows what the problem really is?

Amy clasps my hand. "Listen to me, Charlie. The team needs a different kind of training, that's all. You guys need proper hydration and nutrition. Some altitude simulation training might help too. By the time we play the next game, the whole team will be ready."

She always knows what to do and say. But I need to point out the obvious. "We can't overcome the torpedo bats. The Admirals haven't practiced with those."

"So, we'll practice."

The more I think about the problem, the less certain I am that altitude alone slowed down our best players today. What else could it be? Maybe I'd better talk to Phil and Ray about that.

Chapter Twenty-Eight
The World Series, Part Two

The Admirals won game two, but game three was held at Altitude Stadium. We lost again. The whole team has been doing everything Amy suggested, yet we still can't catch a break. And I can't stop thinking about our bizarre loss of performance—or maybe it's deliberate. Not by our team. But someone who wants to win the World Series badly enough to…I don't know what someone might do.

I glance over at Amy in the dugout, concentration etched on her face as she scribbles something in her notebook. She's been analyzing every play, every swing, studying the Altitude like they're a complex math problem she's determined to solve. Despite our losses, the team respects her for it. Hell, I respect her for it.

"Something's off with our batting," I complain, joining her on the bench. "Nothing helps. It's like we all just get…woozy."

She doesn't look up from her notebook. "You noticed too?"

"Hard not to. Their contact rate is through the roof compared to our regular season matchups."

Finally, she meets my gaze. "I've been tracking their slugging percentage. It's up almost fifteen percent since the playoffs started."

The stadium roars as another Altitude player rounds the bases. I clench my jaw, watching their dugout erupt in celebration.

"Maybe they're just hot right now," I suggest, but I don't believe it. Neither does Amy, judging by the skeptical look she gives me.

"Charlie, when was the last time you saw an entire team suddenly improve this dramatically?" She taps her pen on her notebook. "Something isn't adding up."

I lean forward, elbows resting on my knees, watching their pitcher wind up. "What are you thinking?"

"Not sure yet." She closes her notebook and slides it into her bag. "But I want to check something. After the game, meet me by their equipment room."

I raise my eyebrows. "Are you suggesting we—"

"No sex. Just meet me there." She jumps up, clapping her hands as our next batter approaches the plate. "Let's go, Jackson! Eyes on the ball!"

Three hours later, we've lost 6-2, and the team trudges back to the locker room with slumped shoulders.

I shower quickly, then slip away before the post-game press conference. The hallways underneath Altitude Stadium are a maze of concrete and fluorescent lighting, but I follow the signs toward the home team's area. My heart pounds against my ribs—not from exertion but from the knowledge that we're crossing a line here. If we get caught snooping around the Altitude's equipment room, it'll be more than just embarrassing.

This could end Amy's coaching career before it truly begins.

I find her waiting in a service corridor, her hair still damp from her own shower, dressed in Admirals warm-ups.

"This is crazy," I hiss, glancing over my shoulder. "What exactly are we looking for?"

"I don't know yet." Her voice is hushed yet determined. "But I've been watching baseball my whole life, Charlie. The way you guys have been connecting with the ball isn't natural. The entire team seems almost…drugged."

Oh, shit. I think she's right. It would explain how our entire team could turn into losers overnight. And it's exactly the kind of ploy Jared would concoct.

"Drugged?" I shake my head, but the more I think about it, the more it makes sense. "How would they even pull that off?"

"I don't know yet. That's what we're here to find out."

Amy peeks around the corner, then motions for me to follow. We move silently down the corridor until we reach a door marked "Equipment Storage—Authorized Personnel Only."

"It's probably locked," I whisper.

Amy pulls a keycard from her pocket. "Borrowed this from one of the janitorial staff. Told him I left my tablet in a conference room."

I gape at her. "You're full of surprises, Coach Keller."

"My dad taught me that winning sometimes means thinking outside the rulebook." She swipes the card, and the lock clicks open. "Not cheating—just strategic intelligence gathering."

"You're one sexy spy, Coach."

Her smug smile makes me want to kiss her senseless. But this isn't the right time.

We slip inside the storage room, closing the door behind us. The room is dark until Amy finds a switch, illuminating rows of shelves stacked with equipment. Bats, gloves, helmets, and boxes of balls line the walls.

"What should we be looking for?" I ask, scanning the room.

"Anything suspicious." Amy moves toward the bat rack. "Something that could explain why our team suddenly can't hit worth a damn."

I follow her lead, examining the equipment. The Altitude's prized torpedo bats are arranged neatly on a special rack. They look normal—polished wood, professionally maintained.

"These are our game bats." I run my fingers along one of them. Something feels off about the texture—a slight stickiness to the grip that doesn't seem right. I lift my fingers to my nose and catch a faint, familiar scent.

"Amy," I whisper urgently. "Smell this."

She moves closer, her shoulder brushing against mine as she leans in. Amy takes the bat, brings it up to her nose, and…her eyes widen. "Is that what I think it is?"

"Feels oily and smells like marijuana, so it must be THC oil." My mind races with uncomfortable questions, things I wish weren't true. "They might be coating the bats with THC. When our guys make contact, the residue transfers to their hands, gets absorbed through the skin."

Amy wipes a hand over her mouth, saying nothing for a moment. Then her shoulders sag. "Since you all touch your faces constantly during games…"

"We're getting a mild contact high without even knowing it." I clench my fists. "That's why we all feel woozy after a few innings. Our reflexes slow down, our focus gets shot…"

"Those bastards." Amy pulls out her phone, snapping several quick photos of the bats. "We need evidence. Lots of it."

I grab a torpedo bat, turning it over in my hands to examine it more closely. "Look at this. There's slight discoloration on the grip. It's subtle, but it's definitely been treated with something."

"We need to get a sample." Amy glances around the room, then unzips her bag and pulls out a small evidence collection kit. At my surprised look, she shrugs. "I came prepared."

"Of course you did, baby. You're the smartest person I've ever met."

Using a small scraper, she collects residue from the bat grip into a tiny vial. Her movements are quick and precise, as if she's done this before. Maybe Coach Keller has more secrets than I realized.

"We should check the batting gloves too," I suggest. "If they're coating those, the effects would be even more direct."

"Smart idea."

We move to a locker where batting gloves are stacked in neat piles. She carefully examines a pair, turning them inside out.

"Bingo," she whispers, holding the gloves up. "They've treated these too."

I inch closer to take a look. The interior palms have a faint sheen to them, barely perceptible unless you're looking for it. The pieces are falling into place, and it makes me want to punch something—or someone, preferably the slimeball who did this to our team. The Altitude's sudden improvement, our team's collective slump…it wasn't in our minds. This was deliberate sabotage.

"Jared," I growl. "This has his fingerprints all over it."

Amy collects another sample, securing it in her kit. "We have what we need for now."

Just as she zips her bag closed, voices echo from the hallway. My heart slams against my chest. Amy's eyes widen in panic, and we both freeze, listening intently.

"—checking inventory before we head out." That male voice is unmistakably the smug tone of Jared Morris. "Coach wants the trophy bats packed special for tomorrow, so we'd better do this quick before anyone misses us."

Amy seizes my arm, her fingers digging into my bicep as she drags me toward a storage closet at the back of the room. We squeeze inside just as the door to the equipment room swings open. Through a narrow crack, I can see Jared and one of the equipment managers entering.

"These babies are our secret weapon," Jared laughs, picking up a torpedo bat we'd examined a minute ago. "The Admirals don't stand a chance."

Another male voice chuckles. "Braddock looked like he was swinging underwater today."

I can't figure out who the other voice belongs to. The guy isn't quite mumbling, but I have to listen hard to make out the words.

"Yeah, well, that's what happens when you mess with the best," Jared sneers, twirling the bat. "Plus, our little enhancement doesn't hurt."

I tense, ready to burst out of the closet and confront him, but Amy's grip on my arm tightens. Her eyes flash a warning in the darkness: Not yet.

"You sure this stuff is undetectable?" Jared's accomplice asks.

"Completely," Jared says with smug confidence. "The lab guys say it metabolizes so fast there's no trace after a few hours. By the time anyone might think to test, there's nothing to find. And the beauty is, those idiots don't even know why they're playing so badly."

My jaw clenches so hard my teeth might crack. Amy's breathing is shallow beside me, her body pressed against mine in the tight space. I can feel her heartbeat racing as fast as mine. I'm torn between rage and something else—a fierce admiration for the woman beside me, who figured this out when everyone else was looking in the wrong direction.

Morris's collaborator is packing the bats into a special case, handling them with exaggerated care. "You think they'll ever figure it out?"

"By the time they do, we'll be World Series champions," Jared says with a laugh that makes my blood boil. "Besides, it's not technically illegal. It's just a little…competitive advantage."

They continue gathering equipment, joking about our team's struggles. Every word fuels my anger, but I stay put, knowing we need to leave here with our evidence intact.

Finally, after what feels like hours, they finish their task and head toward the door.

"Let's grab a beer," Jared suggests. "I'm buying. We have a lot to celebrate tonight."

When the door finally clicks shut, I exhale, realizing I've been holding my breath. Amy and I remain frozen for several more seconds, listening for any sign of their return.

"Clear," I whisper, easing the closet door open. "We need to get out of here."

Amy nods, her expression a mix of triumph and fury. "We've got them, Charlie. We've actually got them."

"Not until we can catch Jared and his pal juicing our equipment in the dugout or our locker room."

We slip out of the equipment room, checking both directions before hurrying down the corridor. My mind races with the implications of what we've discovered. This isn't just cheating—it's criminal.

"What's our next move?" I ask once we're safely in a service stairwell. "We can't just accuse them without proof."

Amy holds up her bag. "We get these samples tested immediately. I know a lab that can rush the analysis."

"We've got until the next game to flush out the culprits—meaning Jared and his buddy." I hiss a breath out through my nostrils. "I want him caught red-handed where everyone can see."

Chapter Twenty-Nine

A Controversy Erupts

We had yesterday off, which conveniently gave us time to show our evidence to Ray and Phil. After that, they told us to hold tight and not let on to anyone outside of our team until after they figure out how to handle the situation. Amy has custody of the samples, but we hadn't thought to record Jared's conversation with his buddy last night.

We need more proof. The irrefutable kind.

"Leave it with us," Phil suggests. "We don't want to tip off Jared or his cohort just yet. Better figure out exactly what's going on before we make any serious accusations."

I understand his reasoning, though the idea of Jared continuing to mess with our gear—and maybe even our bodies—makes me want to punch my fist through a wall. I need to confront Jared, but that would alert the bastard that we're onto him.

"What about our bats?" Amy asks, concern evident in her voice. "We can't keep playing with compromised equipment."

Ray rubs his chin. "I've ordered new bats—regular and torpedo. They'll be here tomorrow. Until then, we'll need to be extra vigilant."

"Should we take drug tests?" I ask.

Phil and Ray exchange a look. Then Ray explains, "The THC is probably out of your system already, but just to be safe, we've scheduled tests for the team tomorrow morning. It's mandatory for everyone, though we won't say anything about the marijuana yet."

Amy's brows scrunch up. "Why not? Are you worried that one of our guys might be Jared's cohort?"

"I can't believe that, but it pays to be suspicious of everyone—for now."

"Yeah, we need to be on guard at all times," Phil adds. "Only the four of us will know what's really going on."

"Understood," I say, though my muscles tense at the thought of letting Jared get away with this travesty for even one more day. "But I don't like the idea of that asshole touching our stuff in the meantime."

Amy places her hand on my arm, her touch calming me in a way only she can. "I agree, Charlie. But we have no other options."

"We've got the night game tomorrow," Phil reminds us. "I'll have our equipment managers keep a closer eye on everything, but they won't know why. All we can do is act like normal, like nothing unusual is going on—especially around Jared."

"Fine, I understand." But inside, I'm grinding my teeth and seething with rage.

"And for now," Ray adds, "I'll have our security team review the camera footage from the clubhouse and equipment rooms. If Jared's been tampering with our gear, we might catch him on video."

"That's a solid plan," Amy agrees. "But what if Jared finds a way to hide or destroy the evidence before security can review it? Or his cohort does it? We still don't know who the other man is."

Her question hangs in the air, and I can't help but picture Jared's smug face as he gets away with everything. My fists clench involuntarily.

"We need a trap," I blurt out. "We need to catch him in the act."

Phil raises an eyebrow. "What did you have in mind?"

"Tomorrow, before the night game, we let him think we're not suspicious." I hesitate, hit by the sudden fear that we might be walking into a trap. Are Jared and his buddy that clever? I just don't know. But I trust Ray and Phil. "Amy and I will make a show of leaving our equipment unattended at a specific time. We'll have security watching with cameras, ready to catch whatever he does."

Ray nods slowly. "Not a bad idea. But it's risky."

"If we don't stop him now, what's to prevent him from escalating?"

Ray leans back in his chair, considering my words. "You've got a point, Charlie."

Amy crosses her arms. "I agree, it could get worse. What if he moves beyond THC? What if next time it's something more dangerous?"

The thought knifes a chill through me. I hadn't even considered the possibility.

Phil shuts his eyes briefly, then sighs. "All right. We'll set up a sting operation. But you two need to behave normally around Jared, like you don't have a clue what he's up to. If he suspects anything, this plan won't work."

"I can do that," Amy says confidently. "Behaving normally, I mean."

Maybe she is confident that our plan will work. But I'm not so sure about myself. Every time I see Jared's face, I want to punch it. "I'll try my best. Since I already hated him with a vengeance, he won't be suspicious if I glare at him even harder."

"This is bigger than personal grudges, Charlie," Ray asserts firmly. "This is about the integrity of the game and the safety of our team."

Since there's nothing else we can do right now, Phil and Ray gather the entire team in the locker room. They explain everyone will take a random drug test as a new safety feature or...something. I kinda zoned out while the head honchos were talking, lost in my own thoughts. We all submit to the drug tests. But we won't know the results until after tomorrow's game. I'm hoping like hell that I've sweated out the THC by now.

After team practice, I head back to my apartment, my mind spinning with everything that's happened. I'm barely through the door when my phone vibrates. It's Amy.

"Can I come over?" she asks, sounding hesitant. "I don't want to be alone right now."

"That's understandable. I'll order us some food while you get your fine ass over here."

Twenty minutes later, Amy is sitting cross-legged on my couch, her hair pulled back in a messy ponytail. She picks at the label on her water bottle. "What if we're wrong? What if the culprit isn't Jared?"

I pause, a slice of pizza halfway to my mouth. "The evidence points to him. He had access to our equipment, and we heard him talking about the THC. I'd bet my signing bonus it's him."

Amy wilts against the sofa's back, setting her water bottle on the coffee table. "I know it must be him. It's just…this is serious, Charlie. If we're wrong, we could ruin someone's life."

I wriggle up beside her on the couch, near enough to feel her warmth but not quite touching her. "You're anxious, I get that. I am too. But if we're right and we don't stop him, he could ruin our lives—or worse."

"Yeah, I understand that. But I'm scared," she admits quietly. "Not just about Jared, but about what happens if any of us test positive tomorrow. I've worked so hard to get here, Charlie. What if this is how it all ends? I doubt a disgraced woman coach will get many job offers."

The vulnerability in her voice…it startles me. Amy Keller, the toughest female coach in the MLB, seems uncertain of…everything. I reach out and clasp her hand, giving it a gentle squeeze. "We won't end like this, I promise. Ray and Phil know we aren't responsible. They trust us, and they'll fight for us."

She stares into my eyes, unexpectedly vulnerable in a way I haven't seen before. "You can't promise that, Charlie. Baseball is still a boys' club in so many ways."

I sidle even closer, wrapping an arm around her shoulders. "You need to stop imagining every worst-case scenario. Besides, if the tests come back positive for multiple players, they'll have to investigate further. They can't bench the whole team."

Amy lets her head fall back against the sofa. "God, I hate this feeling of helplessness. I've never let anyone have this kind of power over me before."

"Yeah, I'm feeling the strain too." I scrape my hands through my hair. "Ugh. It's like being back in the minors all over again, waiting for someone else to decide your fate."

We cuddle in silence for a few minutes, the sound of the TV in the background barely registering. Amy's hand is cradled in mine, and I never want to let go. I will need to at some point, obviously, but not yet.

"Charlie, what if we both get kicked off the team?"

I turn to face her. "Then we fight it. We get lawyers. We clear our names."

"And if we can't?"

"Then I guess we'll have to figure out what's next together." The words tumbled out before I could stop them. "Because whatever happens, we stick together—forever."

She snuggles up to me, curling herself tightly into almost a ball. I kiss the top of her head, combing my fingers through her hair. The gesture seems to soothe her.

Then she wriggles free and leaps off the sofa. "I should probably go now."

"Stay with me, Amy." The words came out huskier than I intended. "I mean, it's late, and we've both had a hell of a day."

Amy studies my face, and I can almost see her weighing her options. "Well, we are engaged to be married. So it wouldn't be inappropriate." She yawns loudly. "I'm bushed, anyway. Might as well sleep with my favorite guy beside me."

"I'd really like to sleep with you tonight—just sleep. We shouldn't let this drug-testing thing pull us apart." I lift her hand to my lips, kissing it tenderly. "A good night's rest will rejuvenate us for whatever comes next."

"Well…I've never had much luck resisting you." She finally smiles, almost shyly. "I would love to sleep with you tonight—only sleep—in your arms."

I pick her up and carry her into the bedroom.

Chapter Thirty
Spies 'R Us

Yesterday, we received the results of the drug testing. It was THC that Jared used to dope us. Every player on our team showed signs of marijuana in their system, just enough of it to prove what Amy and I had suspected. None of my teammates know yet what's going on. It's better that way for now. I've got my team's backs, and Amy's on board too. We've been strategizing for hours, huddled in her office with the blinds drawn and voices kept low.

"We need to prove he's tampering with the bats," Amy says. Her usual look of determination is adorable and sexy. "The drug tests are only part of it."

"But we need to catch them red-handed," I remind her. "Got any ideas how?"

She leans back against her chair, slapping her pen down on the desk. A self-satisfied smile curves her lips. "We set a trap. After the game."

"After?" I sit up straighter. "Tell me more, Coach."

"If we blow the lid off the drugging scandal now, Jared won't be able to play."

"You're a genius, Amy." I smack a big, wet kiss on her lips. "But I need to whup him so badly that he'll be humiliated forever—before everyone hears about his cheating."

The plan is simple but risky. We'll leave a batch of our torpedo bats seemingly unattended in the equipment room tonight after everyone's gone. We trust Phil and Ray, so we brought them in on our scheme. They suggested using several wifi spy cameras that also have audio capability. Jared and his cohort won't even see the cameras. Each one is the size of a pea.

While Amy and I are busy on the field, Phil and Ray will be monitoring the feeds from their phones. If anything goes down, Phil will call Amy on her phone. She's keeping it muted but with vibration on.

"I still think I should hide in the equipment room," I tell her, rolling a baseball between my palms.

Amy shakes her head. "Too risky. If Jared spots you, our whole plan falls apart."

She's right, but I hate feeling like I'm not doing enough. This is my team, my career on the line. I've faced fastballs coming at me at ninety-nine miles per hour, but somehow this waiting game feels more dangerous.

"But Amy, what if he doesn't take the bait?"

"He will." She slants forward, her hair falling loose from her ponytail. "Jared's too arrogant not to. He thinks he's untouchable."

There's more than baseball at stake between us, and we both know it. We could get into serious trouble if we're wrong about this.

"Ready?" Amy asks, standing up and smoothing her clothes.

"Baby, I was born ready." I wink so she knows I'm joking, though she's smart enough to figure that out on her own. I set the baseball down and follow her out to the field.

The afternoon practice drags. I'm going through the motions, my mind split between the upcoming game and our trap. Every time I see Jared across the field with his team, I want to run over there and slug him in the gut. He catches me staring and smirks, tapping his bat against the ground. The bastard thinks he's won already.

"Focus, Braddock," Amy calls out from the sidelines. "Eyes on the ball, not the enemy."

She's right. I shake it off and drill the next few hits, sending balls soaring. My teammates whoop and holler, their energy infectious. They have no idea why I'm suddenly locked in, but they feed off it anyway. For a few glorious minutes, I forget about Jared, the marijuana, all of it. I'm just playing ball, the way I used to before this mess.

After practice ends, Amy and I set up our trap, carefully arranging the torpedo bats in the equipment room so they look casually stored. In reality, they're perfectly positioned for the cameras. Phil shows me the feed on his phone—crystal clear video of the entire room from three different angles.

"We'll catch the son of a bitch," he whispers, giving my shoulder a squeeze. "Don't worry."

"Thanks, Phil." His support means more than I can express, and I don't even try to come up with anything better to say. I doubt he expects me to, anyway.

As I head to the locker room to shower, I spot Jared lingering near our dugout, pretending to tie his shoe. My muscles tense, ready for confrontation, but I force myself to keep walking. Any acknowledgment now could tip him off.

In the locker room, I take the longest shower of my life, letting the hot water pound against my shoulders. My mind races through every potential scenario for tonight. What if the cameras fail? What if Jared doesn't take the bait? What if he's already figured out that we're onto him?

I shut off the water and towel myself dry, struggling to silence the noise in my head. As I'm getting dressed, I hear a notification sound, indicating a text—from Amy, no doubt.

All set. Equipment room ready. Dinner?

I text back: *Starving. Where are we going?*

Ten minutes later, we're at a small diner three blocks from the stadium. It's a team favorite, but at this hour, it's nearly empty. Perfect for us to talk without being overheard. Amy sits across from me, nursing a cup of black coffee while I nibble on a meat pie. Neither of us has much of an appetite, but we need to keep our strength up. I gently pester Amy until she finally orders a pastry. Well, that's better than nothing.

"Do you think he'll make his move tonight?" I ask between bites.

She taps her fingernails on her mug, a nervous habit I've noticed before games. "If the pattern holds, yes. They've been drugging our team before home games against the Altitude. Tomorrow's match is too important for him to pass up."

"Oh, I can't wait to see his face when we nail him." The thought of Jared finally getting what's coming to him makes the food taste better.

Amy slants toward me, her voice low. "Remember, we need solid evidence. Video of him applying the THC oil to the bats. Circumstantial stuff won't do."

"Yeah, yeah, I know the drill." I twirl spaghetti around my fork, strictly for something to do. "I can't stop thinking about what will happen after we catch him. This could blow up into a massive scandal." I set my fork down, suddenly less hungry. "The league will investigate. There could be hearings, suspensions."

"One step at a time," Amy says, reaching across the table to touch my hand briefly. "First, we get the evidence. Then, we worry about the fallout."

Her phone buzzes on the table. We both freeze and stare at the thing like it might explode.

She flips it over, reads the screen, and then looks up at me. "It's Phil. Just checking in. Nothing happening yet."

I exhale slowly. "This waiting is killing me."

"Welcome to my world as a coach," she says with a tight smile. "Ninety percent preparation, ten percent real action."

We finish our meal in anxious silence, both checking our phones every few minutes for updates. I've never felt time crawl by so slowly. Every person who walks into the diner makes me jump, as if I'm half-expecting Jared to stroll in and catch us plotting against him.

Finally, Amy pays the bill despite my protests, and we head back toward the stadium. The night air has cooled, stars emerging overhead as we walk side by side, our fingers loosely twined. We're a block from the stadium when both our phones buzz simultaneously. My heart hammers as I fumble to check the message from Phil.

Movement in equipment room. Two figures. Get here now.

Amy and I stare at each other for a split second before breaking into a sprint. We're sprinting toward the stadium. My heart pounds against my ribcage, adrenaline flooding my system like I'm up to bat in the bottom of the ninth. We dash through the players' entrance, our footsteps echoing down the empty corridors.

"Wait," Amy hisses, grabbing my arm as we near the equipment room. "We can't just burst in. We need to be stealthy, like undercover agents for the MLB."

"MIB sounds more like it."

Amy gives me the cutest look of confusion. "M what B?"

"Haven't you ever heard of Men in Black? It was a movie but also a real-life phenomenon involved with UFOs and other weird stuff. MIB is the nickname."

She lifts one brow, also twisting her lips upward too. "I had no idea I was engaged to a conspiracy theorist."

I chuckle. "Gonna dump me now, Coach?"

"Oh, no. You aren't getting away from me that easily."

"Well, you have your quirks too. There's your 'always flush three times' bathroom policy, for instance."

Amy rolls her eyes. "Silence, please."

She's right. If we spook Jared now, he might destroy evidence or come up with some plausible excuse.

"Let's check the feed first," I suggest, pulling out my phone.

The video is crystal clear. Jared and his coconspirator are in the equipment room. I can't see the other person well enough to be sure. They're hunched over our bats, applying something with a small brush. The sight makes my clench my fists hard enough that it hurts.

"That's it," Amy whispers, her face illuminated by the screen's glow. "We've got them."

I start to move toward the door, but Amy grabs my wrist, her grip surprisingly strong.

"Not yet," she murmurs. "Let them finish. The more evidence we have, the better."

I force myself to stay put, watching as Jared meticulously works his way through our bats. He's saying something to his accomplice, but the audio is too faint to catch clearly. Phil texts that he's moving to a position near the back exit in case they try to leave that way.

After what feels like an eternity, Jared straightens up, admiring his handiwork. He's wearing that smug, self-satisfied grin I've seen a thousand times across the plate. He high-fives his accomplice, and they start packing up their supplies. Only then do we get a good look at the other guy. We learned two vital facts tonight. Jared is irrefutably the one doctoring our equipment to drug us.

And his accomplice is one of our own—Coach Adrian Rivera.

Chapter Thirty-One
Braddock vs. Morris

Game seven of the World Series will begin this afternoon. The Admirals will trounce the Altitude. I'm certain of that. Since Jared's team will be using torpedo bats, the Admirals have decided to do the same. Only a select group of our hitters will employ them, and they know they're allowed to use them whenever they want.

The playing field will be level this time, though Jared has no idea why. He thinks our guys are high on dope thanks to his marijuana oil trick.

Prepare to be annihilated, Morris, you evil son of a bitch.

But for now, I'll spend some time with my fiancée to relax and prepare for the game this afternoon. Amy is a phenomenal coach, and she gets me in shape for our face-off with the Assitudes. I feel more ready for this game than for any other in my entire career.

This isn't Altitude vs. Admirals. No, it's good vs. evil.

My guys are the warriors for good. I almost wish I had a sword, like a medieval knight. Maybe a horse too.

A few hours later, it's showtime.

The stadium is packed. Fans from both sides fill every seat, their excitement generating palpable energy. I can spot our fans right away. They wear the standard navy blue and gold of the Admirals, hoisting banners and foam fingers featuring our team. The Altitude fans show their forest green and silver throughout the stands too. Signs for both teams chant and raise foam fingers.

I perform my warmup routine in the dugout, watching Jared do the same out on the field. Our eyes meet, and we both smirk. Morris twirls his torpedo bat with an arrogance that he'll soon regret.

"Don't let him get in your head," Amy reminds me, having sidled up beside me. Her hand rests briefly on my shoulder, firm and reassuring. "Morris is counting on that."

"That reptile can't slither inside my head anymore. I feel good—fantastic, actually."

She studies my face, then her lips curl in a slight smile. "You're ready, Braddock."

The announcer's voice booms through the stadium, and the crowd roars as a familiar name is announced. The batter jogs onto the field, his torpedo bat seeming more like a weapon than sporting equipment.

"And now, batting for the Aspen Altitude, Jared Morris!"

His teammates clap and whistle while Jared acknowledges the crowd with a raised bat.

In the bullpen, Amy gives me a subtle nod that confirms what I know I must do. She mouths, "Destroy Morris."

Okay, maybe she didn't actually say that. I was adlibbing in my head.

The first few innings are a deadlock. Neither team scores, though we come close in the third when Rodriguez nearly clears the wall. The Assitudes' pitcher is on fire, but so is ours. The tension builds with every pitch, every catch, every close call.

In the fifth inning, Jared gets his turn at the plate while I'm on the mound. He taps his torpedo bat against home plate and winks at me.

"Let's see what you've got, Chucky," Morris shouts, loud enough for everyone in the first few rows to hear. "Or are you too busy thinking about your wedding? Maybe you should've picked a different career. Baseball was never really your thing."

I grip the ball tighter, feeling the seams dig into my fingers. Focus. I wind up, delivering a fastball that screams toward the plate, but Jared connects. The crack echoes through the stadium as the ball soars toward left field.

But Rodriguez is there, leaping at the wall, his glove extending just enough to snag it before it clears. The crowd erupts, and I pump my fist as Jared throws his bat in disgust.

"Hey Morris, better luck next time!" I couldn't resist razzing the asshole.

By the seventh inning, we're up by two runs, but the Altitude are threatening with runners on first and third. I wipe sweat from my brow, feeling the stadium's collective breath being held as I face down their cleanup hitter. The torpedo bat in his hands gleams under the lights.

I throw a sinker that dives at the last second. He swings and connects, but it's a weak grounder to short. Martinez scoops it and fires to first for the third out. The crowd explodes as we jog back to the dugout.

"Nice pitch," Amy says, handing me a towel. Her eyes dart to the Altitude dugout where Jared is having an animated conversation with their coach. "They're getting desperate. Morris keeps looking at his watch."

"Probably wondering why we're not falling apart." I gulp down a long drink of water. "His little drug scheme isn't working like he planned. Soon, it'll be time to show him just how fast I can pitch."

"Don't get too cocky."

"I won't, promise."

In the ninth inning, with the score still 2-0 in our favor, Jared steps up to the plate again. Two outs, bases loaded. The perfect dramatic showdown for the World Series finale.

The crowd noise swells to a deafening roar. I swear I can almost feel the vibrations through my cleats as I take the mound. Jared's face is twisted into an expression that seems to mix determination with something else—frustration, maybe even fear. His plan is unraveling, and he knows it.

"This is it, Morris," I mutter under my breath as I receive the ball from the umpire.

Jared points his torpedo bat at me. "You got lucky before, Braddock. Not this time."

I feel the weight of everything on my shoulders—the team, Amy's faith in me, my own redemption. The catcher signals for a fastball. I shake my head. No, I've been setting Morris up all game. It's time for the changeup.

I nod, wind up, and deliver. The ball floats toward the plate, looking like my fastball until the last second when it drops just below Jared's swing. He commits too early, his powerful torso rotating ahead of the ball. Time slows. I see the confusion in his eyes as he realizes he's been fooled. His arms try to adjust mid-swing, the torpedo bat wobbling in his grip.

Too late.

The sound of the ball hitting the catcher's mitt is like thunder in my ears. The umpire's arm shoots up.

"Strike two!"

The catcher hurls the ball back with knife-like precision, and I snag it with a snap of my glove, the sound cracking through the air like a whip. Jared's eyes burn with fury, and his knuckles are clenched tightly around the wooden handle of his torpedo bat. I can almost hear his teeth grinding as he unleashes a menacing growl amid the din of the stadium.

"Problem, Morris?" I goad him, my voice cutting through the tension just enough for him to hear.

He grinds his cleats into the dirt with a force that might almost shake the ground beneath us. The crowd's roar crescendos into a deafening whirlwind, an unstoppable force battering us from all sides. I shut it out, laser-focused on Jared's eyes, the catcher's mitt, and the ball's grip against my fingers as sweat dribbles down the back of my neck.

This pitch has to be flawless, a blazing testament to my determination—and Amy's. I wouldn't be here today, playing the World Series, without her guidance and love. For her, for myself, I will obliterate the fastball records of two legends—Aroldis Chapman and Nolan Ryan—my idols, my benchmarks. I shattered Chapman's record earlier this season. Now, Ryan's hovers in my crosshairs.

I scan the runners, then coil into my windup, a tightly wound spring of potential energy. Time seems to bend as I unleash the ball, a four-seam fastball that screams toward home plate with unrelenting velocity. My arm is a conduit of raw power, a live wire surging with untapped reserves. The ball becomes a blinding comet, a white-hot streak slicing through the air.

Jared swings with everything he has, the torpedo bat whistling. For one unbelievable moment, I think he's going to connect.

But he doesn't.

The ball detonates into the catcher's mitt with such ferocity that he staggers backward a step and almost trips over his own cleats. The stadium plunges into a stunned silence, a collective gasp echoing in the void before the umpire's decisive gesture shatters it.

"Strike three! You're out!"

The stadium explodes into a frenzy with screams and cheers echoing through the stadium with deafening volume. My teammates flood out of the dugout, a tidal wave of navy and gold crashing toward me with unstoppable force. I'm hoisted onto their shoulders, arms thrust skyward in a victorious roar as the announcer's voice thunders through the chaos.

"The Jacksonville Admirals have seized the World Series!"

Through the chaos, I spot Jared. He stands frozen at home plate, the torpedo bat hanging limply at his side. His face is a mask of disbelief and rage, like a man watching his empire of deception crumble before his eyes. I lock onto his gaze for a matter of seconds, and there's a flicker of something—recognition, perhaps, that he's been outplayed.

Then the victory pile engulfs me, bodies pressing in from all sides as my teammates release their unbridled joy with deafening effect. I catch glimpses of the scoreboard flashing our triumph, of fans leaping and embracing, of Amy pushing through the crowd toward me. Her joy shines from every pore.

"You did it!" she virtually shrieks above the pandemonium. She reaches for my hand as I'm lowered back to the ground. "Charlie, that was—"

"I know." Can't believe it myself, but the reality will sink in soon enough. We did it. The Admirals are World Series champions. Still reeling from the news, I drag Amy into my arms and spin her round and round. Once I finally set her down, I have to ask. "Did I smash the fastball record?"

Just then, Phil and Ray come racing out of the dugout toward us. They must have news. Right? But before they can reach us, the announcer tells me what I've been waiting to hear.

"Ladies and gentlemen! Quiet please!"

An eerie hush fills the whole stadium, as if everyone is holding their breath.

"It's just been confirmed!" the announcer declares. He pauses to take a big breath that's audible through his mic. "Charlie Braddock's fastball clocked in at 101.3 miles per hours! It's a new world record!"

Holy shit.

The announcer comes on again. "Sorry, folks, I got so worked up about Charlie's accomplishment that I almost forgot to tell you...the Admirals have won the World Series!"

Chapter Thirty-Two
Winners Take All

The stadium erupts yet again in a new frenzy that seems to vibrate through the air, and my teammates pile on me for a second time. This moment—this perfect, crystal-clear moment—is everything I've worked for since the day I first picked up a bat in Little League. Years of training, of pushing my body to its limits—of weathering slumps, injuries, doubts, and Jared's mind games—everything has led to this, the pinnacle of my career.

"You did it, Charlie!" Amy's voice cuts through the noise, and her eyes shimmer with tears of joy. "You beat them all—Chapman, Ryan, and most importantly, that bastard Morris."

I pull her close, breathing in her familiar scent. "We did it, baby. Couldn't have done it without you."

Over her shoulder, I spot Jared being ushered toward the locker rooms, his shoulders slumped in defeat. Our eyes meet for one final time, and I can't help the surge of satisfaction that courses through me. For years, he's been the thorn in my side that kept pricking me, trying to make me doubt myself. It never worked until the day Jared wrecked my shoulder. But tonight, all the keeps running through my mind is that epic pitch and the roar of victory in my ears. I'm finally free of his shadow.

Jared pauses at the tunnel entrance, his expression unreadable from this distance. Then he's gone, swallowed by the darkness.

"Charlie! Charlie!" The fans are chanting my name in a rhythmic pulse. I raise my hands high, waving as I acknowledge them, letting their energy crash over me.

Coach Rivera claps me on the shoulder. "That was some of the finest hitting I've ever seen, son."

I can't move or speak, still processing what just happened. "The ball…it felt so right."

"It's not the ball," Amy whispers, her fingers twining with mine. "The power was inside you all along."

The team hoists me onto their shoulders, and somebody hands me a torpedo bat that I clutch in my hand like a trophy, raising it high.

"Speech! Speech!" someone shouts, and soon the entire stadium takes up the chant.

I shake my head, laughing. "Put me down, you animals. You know I suck at making speeches."

But they insist, and soon I'm standing on the dugout steps as twilight begins to paint the sky with vivid colors. The floodlights come on, making me squint as I face the sea of blue and white—Admirals colors worn proudly by thousands. Somebody shoves a mic in front of me, ensuring my awkward speech will be heard by everyone.

"I, uh—" My voice cracks, and I clear my throat. "Baseball's always been my language. Not sermons from the mound."

The crowd laughs, patiently waiting.

Amy comes up beside me, handing me a ball, and suddenly, I find the right words. "Eight months ago, I couldn't even grip a ball or a bat without pain shooting up my arm. Some people—including me—thought I was done for." I pause, glancing at the torpedo bat in my left hand and the ball in my right palm. "But this team, this city, and especially this woman right here, they refused to let me believe that."

The crowd shouts their approval as I squeeze Amy's hand. She beams up at me, pride etched across her features.

"Tonight wasn't just about beating Jared Morris." I speak his name clearly, without flinching. "It was about proving that setbacks don't define us. The comeback does."

I survey the faces of my teammates, all grinning like idiots.

"So thank you, Jacksonville. Thank you for believing in me despite what anybody else thinks. And thank you for your unwavering support. Admirals rock!" I raise my ball and holler, "Now, does anybody want to celebrate at Atlantic Beach? I'll buy the piña coladas!"

That garners a laugh, and I feel a weight lift from my shoulders. I raise the bat high one more time, and the crowd goes wild.

As we make our way down the tunnel toward the locker room, I can't stop smiling. The energy in the room is electric, with guys whooping and hollering, spraying champagne like we just won the World Series.

Well, yeah, we did just that. What lucky jerks we are.

"Braddock!" Sanchez calls out, tossing me a bottle. "You magnificent bastard!"

I catch the bottle one-handed, pop the cork with my thumb, and take a swig. The bubbles fizz in my throat, but it's the sweetness of victory that I'm really tasting.

In the corner, Phil is on his phone, his expression shifting from elation to something far less pleasant. He catches my eye and motions me over.

"What's up, boss?" I ask. Phil's never been one to dampen celebrations. That means something must be wrong.

"Just got a call from the league office." Phil keeps his voice hushed. "They need you and Amy in the conference room. Now."

"What? Why?" I glance at Amy, who's laughing with some of the guys near the lockers. "We're celebrating."

Phil rubs his jaw. "It's about Morris and Rivera. And our tainted equipment."

"You mean the marijuana oil scheme."

"Yeah." Phil's gaze darts around as if he's making sure no one else will overhear. "Turns out Morris wasn't just trying to knock you off balance with all that trash talk and secretly drugging you guys. The league's got evidence he was trying to sabotage the team in other ways too."

I feel like I've been hit with a fastball to the gut. "Sabotage? How?"

Phil glances toward the door. "I can't say much here. But remember how our equipment manager found those drilled-out spots in some of our old bats? Turns out it wasn't just wear and tear."

"Son of a—" I cut myself off, my thoughts racing. "Morris did that?"

"The league has video evidence. The pea-size cameras we set up caught him in our equipment room three weeks ago, but nobody looked at the whole footage until now. But now we've alerted the league to Jared's marijuana scheme." Phil's voice drops even lower. "There's more, but we need to keep this quiet until the official announcement. The commissioner wants your statement."

Amy approaches, her victory smile fading as she senses the tension. "What's going on?"

I fill her in quickly, watching her expression shift from confusion to anger. Her hands ball into fists at her sides.

"That cheating bastard," she hisses. "I knew he was desperate, but this? It goes way beyond any team rivalry."

I hold her close as I struggle to process everything we now know. My victory high is still going, but now it's tinged with something else—anger, yes, but also a strange sense of validation. After my injury, I'd wondered if my struggles against Jared were partly in my head, if I was making excuses for not measuring up. But no, he'd actually been sabotaging me, us, the whole team.

I clasp Amy's hand. "Let's go. The sooner we deal with this, the sooner we can get back to celebrating."

We follow Phil down the corridor, away from the noise of the locker room. The concrete hallway feels cold after the warmth of victory, our footsteps echoing against the walls.

"You know," I say, breaking the tense silence, "part of me always suspected something wasn't right. The way our performance would tank against Aspen when we'd been unstoppable the week before against a different team."

"Jared's always been obsessed with beating you," Amy points out.

"Yeah, but drugging us? Sabotaging equipment? That's criminal."

"And it ends tonight," Phil asserts firmly as we approach the conference room. "The league's taking this very seriously."

The door swings open to reveal Commissioner Davis as well as two league officials who are seated at a long table. Their faces are grim. Folders and tablets lay spread out before them. On a screen behind the duo, a video is paused, showing a figure that's unmistakably Jared. He's hunched over what looks like our equipment bags. The video is from the tiny camera Amy and I had installed.

"Mr. Braddock, Ms. Keller," Commissioner Davis says, standing to shake our hands. "Thank you for joining us on such short notice. Please, have a seat."

I slide onto a chair, my body still humming with adrenaline from the game and our incredible win. The leather feels cool against my sweaty back. Amy takes the seat beside me, her posture rigid.

"First, congratulations on your performance tonight," Davis tells us. His tone is professional, but I detect genuine touch of admiration. "That was some impressive pitching."

"Thank you, sir," I respond, my eyes drifting to the frozen image on the screen. "But I'm guessing we're not here to discuss my batting average."

Davis releases a long sigh, then presses a button that brings the video to life.

The recording plays, and there he is—Jared Morris in our equipment room at two a.m., methodically working on our bats. He has a bottle of marijuana oil in his hand. Well, I assume that's what it is. The jerk methodically applies the oil to every bat, every ball, every glove—as if to ensure not one player would be unaffected by his tampering.

But Jared isn't alone. He has a friend with him, though it's not who I expected.

I lean forward, my body tense as I strain to make out the other figure in the shadows. The grainy security footage plays on, and I feel my stomach drop as the individual steps into the light. Then a name tumbles from my lips. "Coach Rivera?"

Amy gasps beside me, her hand finding mine under the table and squeezing hard. My heart pounds like a bass drum in a marching band.

"I'm afraid it's true," Commissioner Davis confirms, his expression grim. "Shawn Rivera has been working with Morris for the past season and a half. Morris had blackmail material that he'd been holding over Rivera, something to do with him unknowingly hiring underage prostitutes. That's no excuse for what he helped Morris do. But only during the playoffs did they come up with a workable plan to foul up the Admirals chances at reaching the World Series."

The video continues playing. Rivera is carefully applying the marijuana oil to the gloves while Jared applies the substance to the bats. They work with practiced efficiency, as if they've done this many times before.

"Son of a bitch," I mutter, anger rising inside me, as hot as molten metal. "He was in the dugout with us, celebrating tonight. Patting me on the back, telling me how proud he was." I shake my head, disgust and betrayal warring within me. "But the whole time, he must've been laughing on the inside."

"Both Morris and Rivera have been taken into custody," Davis explains. "The evidence is overwhelming. Not just this video, but text messages, bank transfers showing payments from Morris to Rivera, and testimony from an equipment manager who became suspicious."

Amy leans forward, her coach's instincts kicking in. "What about the game tonight? Does this invalidate our win?"

"No," Davis confirms. "Your victory stands. In fact, it makes what you accomplished even more impressive. You were playing against a stacked deck and still came out on top."

I let out a breath I didn't realize I was holding. "And the marijuana oil? That's why half of our guys were acting so strangely during practices?"

"Precisely. Slow reflexes, decreased coordination, impaired judgment—all symptoms your team was experiencing," Davis pinches the bridge of his nose, shutting his eyes for a few seconds. Then he looks at us. "The oil was absorbed through the skin. They were essentially drugging you without your knowledge."

I push a hand through my hair, which is still damp with sweat from the game. "Damn, I can't believe it. Coach Rivera was always so helpful and…nice."

Amy rests her cheek on my shoulder. "He fooled us all, Charlie. It isn't your fault."

I scratch my neck, still trying to process this information. "No wonder I couldn't connect properly in our last series against the Altitude." I shake my head. "All the missed opportunities, the frustration, the self-doubt that plagued me. I thought I was just in a slump."

But no, my game wasn't off. Jared Morris and Adrian Rivera conspired against me and the whole Admirals team.

Shit. At least it's over now.

Chapter Thirty-Three
The Off Season

After a few days of rest, Amy and I get a visit from Phil and Ray that might end our mini vacation. They've both decided that I "absolutely must" go on a publicity tour to promote my record-setting fastball pitch—and also to promote the team's World Series win. I hoped it might be a low-key thing. But no, Ray and Phil insist on a whirlwind event complete with photographers, reporters, and magazine write-ups.

The crazy train is about to leave the station.

"It'll be a three-city tour," Phil explains as we sit in my living room. "Jacksonville, New York, and Los Angeles. Maximum exposure."

I rub my temples, already feeling a headache forming. "How long will this tour be?"

"Two weeks," Ray says, checking his phone. "We've already booked everything. The team's PR department has set up interviews with ESPN, Sports Illustrated, and a dozen local stations in all three venues."

Amy, sitting beside me on the couch, places her hand on my knee. The subtle gesture is comforting. "Let's not overwork our star player. He might reinjure his arm. After all, you did mention having him replicate his record-setting fastball multiple times in different venues."

"Charlie's arm will be fine," Ray interrupts, glancing up from his phone. "The doctors cleared him. Besides, he won't be pitching—just talking. Smiling for cameras. Signing some baseballs."

I glance at Amy, whose nostrils are flaring. I know that look well. It's her I'm-about-to-say-something-that-might-cost-me-my-job expression. "With all due respect, Ray, Charlie's recovery has been miraculous, but he's not invincible. We need to be strategic about his public appearances."

Ray lifts his brows. "Are you suggesting we cancel the tour, Coach Keller?"

"No," she replies evenly. "I'm suggesting we modify it. Cut it to one week, focus on quality over quantity, and make sure Charlie has adequate rest between events."

I clear my throat. "I appreciate everyone's concern, but I should probably have some say in this, right?"

Three pairs of eyes turn to me expectantly.

"Look, I understand the importance of publicity. I get that this is part of the job. But I also need to make sure I'm ready for next season. So, Amy's compromise does sound reasonable to me."

Phil puckers his lips, tapping one finger on his knee. "One week could work. We'd have to consolidate some interviews, but—"

"Absolutely not," Ray interjects. "This tour is about capitalizing on momentum. One week isn't enough time to hit all the markets properly."

I throw my head back and groan. "Ugh. Ray, I respect you as an owner, but this is my body we're talking about. My career. I came back from an injury that nearly ended everything, and I don't want that to happen again."

The room falls silent for just long enough that I'm starting to get worried. "Tell you what. Let's shoot for ten days. We'll hit all three cities, but we schedule in proper rest days. And no demonstration pitches unless I feel one hundred percent."

Ray studies me for a long moment, his expression unreadable. Then he sighs, nodding in resignation. "Fine. Ten days it is, with rest periods built in." He points a finger at me. "But I want your A-game when you're on camera. The fans want to see Charlie Braddock, not some exhausted shadow of him."

"You'll get my best," I vow. "Every time, rain or shine."

Phil scribbles notes on his tablet. "I'll rework the schedule tonight. We leave in three days."

Once big guys are gone, Amy and I collapse back onto the couch.

She curls into my side, her head resting on my shoulder. "That went better than expected, huh?"

I laugh, but the sound feels hollow even to my ears. "Yeah, Ray only looked like he wanted to fire me twice."

"He wouldn't dare. You're the golden boy right now. Record-breaking fastball, remember?" She wriggles closer, lowering to a sexy register. "Besides, I think you handled that perfectly. You stood your ground without burning bridges."

"Ten days is better than two weeks. We also have our wedding coming up, ya know. Our moms won't be happy if we cut the nuptials short."

"We won't skimp on the wedding craziness. But first, we do the publicity tour. Agreed?"

"As long as you're coming with me, baby, I'll go anywhere."

She smiles, that special smile she reserves just for me. "Someone has to make sure you don't overdo it. Besides, I'm your coach. It's literally my job to monitor your physical condition."

I pull her close, planting a kiss on her forehead. "So, you're coming as my coach, not my fiancée?"

"Both." She traces a finger along my jaw. "Always both."

That night, I lie awake staring at the ceiling. Amy's delicate breathing beside me is the only sound in the room. Can I make it through ten days of being paraded around like a prized racehorse? Ten days of repeating the same stories, answering the same questions about how it felt to throw that pitch, how it felt to win the Series? The press will also want to talk about the arrests of Coach Rivera and Jared Morris.

I shift around on the mattress, careful not to wake Amy. What if Ray pushes too hard? What if I can't say no when some hotshot reporter asks me to demonstrate my famous fastball for the twentieth time? What if—

"I can hear you thinking," Amy murmurs, her voice thick with sleep. She rolls over, propping herself up on one elbow. In the dim light filtering through the blinds, I can make out her concerned expression. "What's going on in that head of yours?"

I sigh, turning to face her. "It's nothing. Just some pre-tour anxiety. Cameras. Questions. People expecting me to be awesome at all times."

She grazes her lips over mine, speaking in a sultry tone. "But you are awesome, twenty-four seven."

I hesitate, considering what she said. Then I sigh and shake my head. "You're absolutely right. I shouldn't have let midnight doubts creep in. My fastball set a record. I've got nothing to worry about."

And I mean that. Amy is the most amazing coach and the most amazing woman.

In three days, the publicity tour will begin. But apparently, I have momentous decisions to make in the meantime.

"You need new clothes," Amy declares over breakfast, scrolling through her phone while I shovel cereal into my mouth.

"What's wrong with my clothes?" I ask around a mouthful of Frosted Flakes.

She gives me a look that could wilt flowers. "Charlie, you have exactly two dress shirts that fit properly, and that navy suit you wore to the awards dinner has seen better days."

I glance down at my current outfit—gym shorts and a faded Admirals T-shirt with a small hole near the collar. "Fair point."

Shopping isn't my favorite activity, but Amy makes it bearable. We hit the upscale men's store downtown where a salesman named Marco fusses over me like I'm royalty. Two hours later, I've got three new suits, five dress shirts, and a pair of shoes that cost more than my first car. Marco insists the navy suit is a "timeless classic" that will photograph well on camera.

Amy's gaze travels over me while I model the final ensemble. "You look like a million bucks."

I adjust my sleeve cuffs. "I'm more concerned about pleasing *you*."

She steps closer to straighten my tie. "Mission accomplished, then."

Once we're home, I find a detailed itinerary in my email. The schedule is packed tight—morning shows, radio interviews, photo shoots, fan meet-and-greets, charity events. Even with the compromise of the ten-day timeline, it still looks exhausting.

I scroll through the endless list of commitments. "This is intense."

Amy peers over my shoulder at my laptop. "Ray wasn't kidding about maximum exposure. There's barely time to breathe between these events." She commandeers my laptop, her coach-face settling in as she studies the schedule. "Hmm. The rest periods we asked for are technically there, but they're minimal. And look—they've got you doing a pitching demonstration at Dodger Stadium on day eight."

"I can do that. Don't worry about me."

As she scrolls through the list, her frown deepens. "And here, on day five in New York, they've got you scheduled for a 'friendly competition' with some Yankees relievers. That wasn't part of our agreement."

"I want to do everything that's asked of me. But I hope there'll be some events with kids too."

Amy scrolls a bit more, then points to the screen. "Actually, there are a few kids' events. You'll be visiting a children's hospital in Jacksonville and a youth baseball clinic in Los Angeles." She freezes for a second, then breaks into a wide grin. "Look, Charlie, August Murphy will be there for the Jacksonville event."

"That's fantastic! I've been texting with him, but it'll be fun to see August in person again. His mom says his cancer is in total remission."

I love working with kids—their enthusiasm, their unabashed joy for the game. It reminds me of why I fell in love with baseball in the first place.

Chapter Thirty-Four
The Wedding Night

The last ten days have been a whirlwind, with cameras flashing and reporters shouting questions. The publicity tour went better than I expected. Now that we're home, the press still can't get enough—radio shows, TV spots, newspapers, the works. It was as if the moment I landed back in Jacksonville, the whole city lit up. There's a huge buzz in the media about my return to the Jacksonville Admirals.

We hit all the sports networks, all the local stations, every one hungry for the scoop on my return. They seemed to play up the rivalry drama between our team and the Altitude. But the buzz is real, and it's thrilling. No awkward questions about my past. It feels like the entire baseball world is watching, waiting to see what happens next. They've got a bad case of fastball fever, and I'm loving every second of it.

Naturally, I'm often asked about the marijuana oil scandal surrounding Morris and Rivera.

Because the criminal cases are still pending, I can't say too much. I keep my answers bland and professional, deflecting with practiced ease. The media vultures are always hungry for a juicy soundbite, but I've learned my lesson about running my mouth off.

"Just focusing on baseball" has become my go-to phrase.

I wonder how the Altitude team will make do without Jared Morris. They've got plenty of good players on their side, and none of them knew anything about Morris and Rivera's vicious little scam. I'm sure they'll be fine.

But today, I have a wedding to attend. The groom is kind of necessary, so I'd better get ready. Never would I ever leave Amy waiting at the altar.

I adjust my bow tie in the mirror, feeling anxious and excited simultaneously. Never thought I'd be the kind of guy to get nervous on his wedding day, but I am. The tux fits perfectly, hugging my shoulders in a way that makes me seem quite respectable.

"You clean up decent, Braddock," says a voice from the doorway.

My best man, Teddy Freeman, leans against the frame, dressed and ready to go. Yeah, we've become good buddies—and I'm sure he and Alicia will tie the knot soon too. My sister Kaitlyn has just started dating one of my teammates, Danny Alvarez, and I'd bet my signing bonus there will be another Admirals wedding before long. Danny's a great guy, and I approve wholeheartedly.

Teddy tosses me a small velvet box. "Don't lose the rings, Braddock, or Coach Keller will have both our asses."

I chuckle, but my hands tremble slightly as I pocket the box. "She's not my coach anymore."

"Nah, now she's your boss for life."

We share a grin, and I turn back to the mirror. It's strange how life works out. Once, I was a player with a bad shoulder who felt washed-up and expected zero prospects. Now I'm marrying the woman who not only fixed my career but stole my heart in the process.

"You nervous?" Teddy asks, coming to stand beside me.

"Nah, of course not." My palms are sweating, though, and there's a flutter in my stomach that makes my pre-game jitters seem like nothing. "Not about marrying Amy, that is. It's the easiest decision I've ever made. But to stand there in front of everyone..."

Teddy claps a hand on my shoulder. "The Charlie Braddock I know isn't afraid of a crowd. You play in front of thousands every week."

"Yeah, but I know what I'm doing on the mound. This is different."

"Just think of it as another game. Eyes on the prize, man."

The prize. That's Amy Keller. Soon to be Amy Braddock.

My best man leads me out of the room, and we make our way through the hotel hallway. My family booked the entire top floor of Jacksonville's fanciest hotel for the reception. My parents spared no expense, probably because they never thought they'd see the day their troublemaker son would settle down.

"You got your vows?" Teddy asks as we wait for the elevator.

I pat my breast pocket. "Right here. Though I might just wing it."

"Don't you dare," he warns. "Amy will kill you."

"Relax, I'm kidding." The paper in my pocket has some bullet points, but I've never been good at reading from a script. What I feel for Amy can't be contained in carefully crafted sentences. It's wild and messy and perfect—just like our journey together.

The elevator doors open, and we step inside. My stomach drops as we descend, and it's not just the motion causing the swooping sensation in my gut. This is happening. I'm about to marry the most incredible woman I've ever known.

"You are going to crush this, Charlie." Teddy checks his watch. "Just like game seven against the Altitude last season."

I smile at the memory. Bottom of the ninth, bases loaded, two outs. Amy had prepped me for that exact scenario. "Minus the fastball to the face of their cleanup hitter."

Teddy laughs. "I think Morris deserved it after what he said about your arm."

The elevator doors glide open, revealing the hotel's grand lobby. It's been transformed for the occasion—white flowers everywhere, ribbons draped from the ceiling, and a small army of photographers ready to capture every moment. The Admirals' PR crew insisted on having exclusive photos for the team website, and I didn't have the heart to say no. Being the face of the franchise comes with its perks and its obligations.

"Showtime," Teddy whispers.

I spot my sister Kaitlyn waving frantically from across the lobby. She's stunning in her bridesmaid dress, a soft blue that complements her eyes—the same shade as mine, a Braddock family trait.

"Charlie!" Katie rushes over, nearly tripping in her heels. "You look incredible! Amy's going to flip when she sees you."

"How is she?"

My sister grins. "Calm as can be. You know Amy. She's treating this like another game day. Said something about 'executing the plan' and 'staying focused on the objective.'"

That sounds exactly like my Amy. Always the coach, even on our wedding day. Knowing Amy is approaching our wedding with her usual steady determination calms me in a way nothing else could. It's one of the countless reasons I love her.

My parents appear, Mom already dabbing at her eyes with a handkerchief. Dad looks uncomfortable but proud in his tuxedo, his hand resting on Mom's back.

"Son," Dad says, extending his hand to me. When I take it, he pulls me into a surprising hug. "You did good. She's a keeper."

"I know, Dad."

Mom fusses with my boutonniere, straightening it unnecessarily. "Your grandfather would have loved to be here. He always said you'd find your way."

Grandpa Braddock was the one who first put a baseball in my hand when I was just a kid. He'd played minor league ball himself, never quite making it to the majors, but his passion for the game was infectious. I wish he could see me now—not just because I've made it to the big leagues, but because I've found someone who believes in me the way he did.

Teddy checks his watch. "It's time."

We make our way to the hotel's garden terrace where the ceremony will take place. The late afternoon sun casts a golden glow over everything, and a gentle breeze carries the scent of jasmine and sea salt from the nearby coast. It's perfect—elegant but not stuffy, just like Amy wanted.

I step up to the altar, trying not to fidget as guests fill the rows of white chairs. I spot several of my Admirals teammates, all looking uncharacteristically polished in their suits. Even Phil and Ray are here, looking more comfortable than I would've expected. Those guys were the ones who insisted Amy should take me on as a special project back when my career was circling the drain. Phil saw something in me that I'd forgotten was there.

The string quartet begins to play, and my heart rate doubles. I wipe my palms on my pants, earning a sarcastically disapproving look from Teddy.

"Dude, keep it together," he murmurs.

"I'm trying," I mutter back.

The bridesmaids begin their procession, each one more beautiful than the last. Kaitlyn winks at me as she takes her place opposite Teddy. Then the music changes, and everyone rises.

And there she is.

My bride appears at the end of the aisle, her arm linked with my father's. Her dress is simple but stunning, hugging her athletic figure before flowing out around her feet. Her hair is swept up elegantly, a few tendrils framing her face. She looks like an angel, all grace and calmness. Amy smiles directly at me with that same focused look she gets when she's calling plays from the dugout. It's a look that says she sees exactly what she wants and knows how to get it.

My nervousness evaporates, replaced by a certainty so profound it feels like I'm standing on the mound with a perfect grip on my fastball. This is where I'm supposed to be.

Amy glides toward me, every step purposeful and graceful. When she reaches the altar, my father kisses her cheek and places her hand in mine.

She winks. "Hey, slugger."

I smile. "Hey, Coach."

Her hand is warm in mine as we turn to face the officiant. The world narrows to just us—me and Amy in this perfect moment.

"Dearly beloved," the officiant begins, but his words blur as I gaze at Amy's profile. The determined set of her jaw, the slight curve of her lips, the way the sunlight catches her hair—I'm memorizing every detail. When it's time for vows, I reach into my pocket for the paper, but something stops me. I let my fingers slip away from the carefully written words.

I gaze directly into her eyes and speak from the heart. "Amy, I had this whole speech prepared. But standing here looking at you, I realize no script could capture what I feel for you. I came to you broken—a pitcher who'd lost his confidence, his fastball, and his way. But you saw something worth saving. You pushed me harder than anyone ever has, believed in me when I couldn't believe in myself."

I take a moment to gather my remaining thoughts, but Amy doesn't seem to mind the small delay. As I gaze deeply into her eyes, I can feel her love like a palpable force. I give her hands a light squeeze.

"Before you, baseball was just about me—my stats, my career, my ego. You taught me it's about something bigger. It's about trust and teamwork and fighting for something together." I suck in a breath, releasing it in a rush. "That's what I'm promising you today. To be your teammate in everything. To have your back in every inning of our life together."

A tear slides down Amy's cheek, but her smile never wavers. That's my coach—emotional but unbreakable.

"I love you, Amy Keller. Not just because you saved my career, but because you made me want to be better—as a player and as a man."

Amy's eyes shine with unshed tears, but her voice is unwavering as she begins her vows. Pure Amy, composed under pressure. She twines her fingers with mine. "Charlie Braddock, when the team brought you in, I saw a pitcher with a million-dollar arm and a ten-cent head."

The crowd laughs, and I can't help but join them. It's true.

"I thought I could fix your mechanics. I never expected you to fix my heart." Her voice softens. "I've spent my life studying the science of this game—velocity, spin rate, release points. But loving you? That defies all analysis. "You taught me that sometimes the most beautiful plays aren't the ones you diagram on a clipboard. They're the ones that happen when you trust someone enough to improvise."

Suddenly, I've got a lump in my throat. But it feels…good.

Amy's lip curl into the sweetest smile. "I promise to be your biggest fan and your toughest critic. To celebrate your wins and help you through the losses. To build our team—our family—with the same dedication we bring to the field every day. And I promise never to call time out when the game gets tough."

The officiant seems genuinely moved. "The rings, please."

My best man hands them over, and I slide the simple platinum band onto Amy's finger right in front of the engagement ring. She slips my ring on, tears glistening in her eyes. The weight of the ring feels right, like the perfect grip on a baseball—something that belongs there.

"By the power vested in me," the officiant says, "I now pronounce you husband and wife. You may kiss the bride."

I don't hesitate. I haul Amy into me, one hand at her waist, the other cradling her face. Our lips collide, and the crowd erupts in cheers and applause. I can pick out the distinct whoops and hollers of my teammates, who aren't exactly known for their subtlety.

When we finally peel our lips apart, Amy says, "Nice execution, Braddock."

"I had a great coach."

We whirl around to face our guests as the officiant exclaims, "Ladies and gentlemen, I present to you Mr. and Mrs. Braddock!"

We walk down the aisle hand in hand, showered with flower petals and cheers. The reception flows by in a blur of champagne toasts, cake cutting, and first dances. Amy moves with the same precision on the dance floor as she does in the dugout, following my lead with an ease that makes me look better than I am.

She licks a bit of frosting from my lips. "You're not half bad at this dancing thing, Mr. Braddock."

"I've been practicing. Didn't want to embarrass myself in front of my coach."

Her laughter is like a perfect pitch—clean, precise, and it hits me right in the heart.

Later, as the night winds down, we find a quiet moment on the balcony overlooking Jacksonville's twinkling skyline. The St. Johns River shimmers in the moonlight, reminding me of all those late-night runs I used to take when I was trying to get my arm back in shape.

I slide my arm around her waist. "Happy, Mrs. Braddock?"

Amy leans into me, her head resting against my shoulder. "Beyond happy. Though I'm already thinking about spring training."

I grin, because of course she is. "Can't we enjoy the honeymoon first?"

She laughs. "I suppose I'll allow that."

My sister Lauren appears at the edge of the balcony. "Come on, you two. It's time to start your honeymoon—if either of you will tell us where you're going. You've been awfully secretive about it."

We let Lauren shepherd us away from the balcony and back to the main reception area. Then my sister shoves two fingers in her mouth to issue an earsplitting whistle. "Listen up, folks! Charlie and Amy will now reveal their honeymoon destination."

My bride and I exchange glances and shrugs.

Kaitlyn rushes up to us. "Please tell us. It must be someplace glamorous."

"Okay, okay, we'll tell you." I look at Amy just as she looks at me, and I know we're thinking the same thing. In unison, we shout, "Cooperstown, of course!"

Everyone laughs and cheers.

We'll do the Caribbean thing for our first anniversary. But baseball is in our blood, and there's no place we'd rather start our marriage than in Baseball's Hometown.

Anna Durand is a bestselling, multi-award-winning author of contemporary and paranormal romance. Her books have earned bestseller status on every major retailer and wonderful reviews from readers around the world. But that's the boring spiel. Here are the really cool things you want to know about Anna!

Born on Lackland Air Force Base in Texas, Anna grew up moving here, there, and everywhere thanks to her dad's job as an instructor pilot. She's lived in Texas (twice), Mississippi, California (twice), Michigan (twice), and Alaska—and now Ohio.

As for her writing, Anna has always invented stories in her head, but she didn't write them down until her teen years. Those first awful books went into the trash can a few years later, though she learned a lot from those stories. Eventually, she would pen her first romance novel, the paranormal romance *Willpower*, and she's never looked back since.

To get exclusive content, join Anna's Facebook group, Anna's Romance Addicts, or sign up for her newsletter.

VISIT ANNADURAND.COM TO SIGN UP.

www.ingramcontent.com/pod-product-compliance
Lightning Source LLC
Chambersburg PA
CBHW072132300726
48975CB00003B/1037